At the Community College:
Smiles and Reflection

Jeffrey Ross, EdD

Preface by
Graham Jones, Community College Student

Forward by
Dr. John Paddison, Professor Emeritus

Special Random After-Stories by
Jann M. Contento PhD
David Forrester, Pastor at Wings of Life Worship Center
John Paddison, PhD
Courtney Rene, Novelist

Published by Rogue Phoenix Press
Copyright © 2019
ISBN: 978-1-62420-426-5

Cover by Designs by Ms G

Dr. Jones' Office
Dr. Hill's Student
Five Good Reasons to Complete that AA Degree
@ Diners Grove
Community Colleges: Exporting Middle Class Dreams
@ Tri-Campus Central College
@ Copperfield High School–Home of the Copperheads
A Shape Shifter Goes to College

Preface

As small children, we have the drive to use our lives to become something miraculous–like the incredible urge to explore the stars as an astronaut. Satisfying the urge to help others might drive someone to the choice to become a doctor or nurse. A kid that enjoys history or arguing with a brother or sister might head to the courtroom to become a lawyer. Some of the greatest celebrities and personas–like Tom Hanks, Nolan Ryan, Steve Jobs, and George Lucas–were all community college graduates. They all, in one way or another, transformed the world with each movie, each pitch, each invention, and each universe they created or influenced.

After some digging, which all of us inevitably do, I concluded that higher education is a necessary part of the journey to achieve future success. But how does an ordinary student reach this goal of higher education? The only way is to balance good grades, pass standardized testing, participate in clubs, sports, activities, and still enjoy a social life. Then, it comes to choosing a college: one of the biggest and most challenging choices of a young person's life. Community colleges provide a journey with hands-on guidance for a substantially reduced cost compared to the major universities. Community colleges allow lost souls, punk kids, and many others to beat out their own paths and find their own truths.

For most, community college is the first step outside the realm of childhood memories and pastimes and the beginning of adult life. College is a place where you can get the first breath of freedom and take the first step outside the shadow of parents or older siblings. Students embrace this new-found light and finally see themselves. For example, introverted young adults, forced to speak in front of the class for the first time, might break out of their shells and grow. Through an art class, they might find new love in the eyes of the *Mona Lisa*. Equations, jumbled to some, might open the mind of a young student to inspire her inner engineer. Community college provides an essential stepping stone from high school to the brave new world of modern society.

Proud professors and dubious doctors roam the luminescent halls and classrooms of these schools to sculpt students' hearts and minds. The staff gently holds the hands of the new students—even though sometimes they slip. Dedicated professors wade through the intricate web of regulations and thesis statements to create lessons plans of substance. They deliver lectures that will stir the minds of future generations (or future dropouts). Administration tirelessly supports, guides, and advises students toward a future they may not even recognize yet.

Community college provides the growth needed to for anyone to develop a personalized education plan. Such colleges provide a safe place for self-exploration. All the while, students juggle sports, work, family, and other activities.

Dr. Ross' collection of enlightened stories about the seldom-recognized ins-and-outs of the community college structure both amuse, delight, shock, and bewilder. Enhanced by the rugged beauty of the southwest, and through an eccentric and quirky set of characters, these stories maneuver the landscape of the sometime-stagnant world of community college administration, staff, and students. They demonstrate the folly of the human condition with humorous stories of the "typical" community college experience through the eyes of all parties involved. Using the extremes of the typical, and the elaborate mazes of the norm, Dr. Ross expresses the pitfalls and successes of the system he dedicated his life to.

Graham Jones, Community College Student.
Gilbert, Arizona
March 15, 2019

Foreword

Throughout our social evolutionary development, the concept of individual identity has been a vital part of the human experience: self, group, tribe, country, institution...whatever the social organization or construct. And as Dr. Ross so artfully demonstrates in the following collection of stories, education is one particular area of identity establishment that remains most troublingly prominent.

Certainly, since Medieval times, the University has been the bastion and repository of "education" and thus, over time, has become the method through which collected knowledge was made transcendent between one generation and the next. And given the old adage that "knowledge is power," over time the educational process become an institutional process for wealth and power reification, while at the same time being a solid method of social exclusion. But let us take a moment to unpack that phenomena, as understanding this differentiation process is crucial to appreciating the richness of the writing contained within Dr. Ross' collection of vignettes.

With its wealth of resources, as well as its democratic underpinnings, America is probably the best place to see the processes of wealth accumulation and social determinism, as well as the ensuing educational identity confusion, taking place. Afterall, consider the Jeffersonian notation that for a democracy to remain vital and transcendent, it must have an enlightened, well informed electorate. The university/four-year college system, which certainly meets Jefferson's demand, was already entrenched in the American society. However, a majority of American citizenry fell far below the high bar of democratic participation and literacy. Eventually, a robust public education system was born to meet this need.

Grades 1 through 8, "primary education," was the mainstay of the literacy efforts in the 18th and 19th centuries, until major economic changes of the times required an additional four years of "secondary education": grades 9 through 12. The primary/secondary school arrangement fit well, and the majority of United States citizens were given basic and trade education, while the exclusivity of the university/four-year college system remained intact. The post-secondary structure of four, then six, then eight years of extended education allowed the time necessary for the preparation of the upper-class and aristocratic class students to acquire the abilities needed to handle and pass on the wealth bestowed on them by the nature and inheritance of their unique birth right and class identity...the mantle of power and privilege and leadership...the identity of the "best and the brightest."

But somehow, democratic social principles could not coexist with the illusion of "*nobles oblige,*" especially after the rape and pillaging of the plebian lower working classes in the ironic period called the Industrial Era. An innovative educational construct, called the "junior college," was meant to somehow bridge the gap between mandatory, publicly paid-schooling, and privately sponsored college education. Later, the "junior college" was euphemistically call the "technical institution," "trade college," "technical trade college," and finally "community college."

Unfortunately, the appellations "junior" and "technical" and "institution," as well as the folksier nominalizers of "city" and "community," gradually attached a negative and subaltern association to the term "college."

During the subsequent years, in order to maintain the mantle and image of the penultimate egalitarian institution, the purpose of the community college truncated into the following: Open access to postsecondary education; Preparation for transfer to four-year college or university; Workforce development and vocational skills training; A range of noncredit programs; and Community enrichment programs and cultural activities. In more recent years, these five basic goals have been reworded and reworked into various verbose and flowery mission and goals statements, but they still remain confusingly similar...an unattainable Desiderata that claims to be all things to all people.

And so, this emergent, contradictory, almost schizoid identity that the has entrapped the two-year community college lo these many decades...this perplexing dilemma... is the focus of the delightful fictional chapters contained in Dr. Ross' collection.

The reader will enjoy this slice-of-life perspective of the most eclectic of American educational institutions. Characters representing the entire community college "Chain of Being" will entertain and enlighten you–and you will hear about the complex community college event from those not always given voice. Read this book to be entertained and to be informed. You won't be disappointed.

P.S. Bye the bye...while the community college still struggles with its identity crisis, four-year institutions have been able to maintain their gatekeeping role by continually raising tuition and costs, while at the same time facilitating the student loan process by which non-privileged students accumulate massive debt in their educational pursuits. The more things change, the more they remain the same...

Dr. John Paddison
Gold Canyon, Arizona
May 1, 2019

The Stories for Smiles and Reflection

A Community College Professor's Reflections

@Southern New Mexico Bright Wall Community College

Joey Archbishop, PhD, was at that time of life when a man begins to reflect on the significant events and themes of his life–and how those events and themes shaped him. He had never been a good student in high school, but persevered and graduated without too much trouble. He was never really an athlete, but as a kid, he enjoyed riding motocross bikes in the New Mexico desert–and working on two-stroke engines.

When he was sixteen or so, his career ambition was to work in a motorcycle shop–but his parents would hear nothing about such an idea. They wanted him to go to college and "make something" out of himself. So, through a strange pathway of junior college, college, and a couple of universities–and stopping out and dropping out a few times, he ended up with a career as a community college English professor. He held a PhD in American Lit (Whitman), but most of his work life had been spent teaching 100-level ENG composition courses. Dr. Joey had read so many essays, graded so many papers, attended so many division meetings.

His dad had given him some simple advice, all those years ago, which turned out to be invaluable: "Just get a degree in something. Anything. You will be better off with a degree." So, Archbishop, after a few starts and stops, became an English major. Reading books and writing about them seemed easy, and interesting, to the young beer-drinking scholar. He ended up having forty-eight credit hours of English for his BA, thirty-six for his MA, and another forty-five for the doctorate. Not always as easy as he hoped, but he had it all done by the time he was thirty-one. He didn't even have to borrow too much money back then.

Archbishop always enjoyed living "close to the bone." Besides, as his academic life progressed, he found he enjoyed reading poems by Roethke or novels by Updike more than going to movies, football tailgate parties, or expensive restaurants. You might say he had different priorities – especially as the literature he studied began to impact his own thinking and values.

Both perseverance and chance landed him on the full-time faculty at SNMBWCC. After spending five unsteady years in college and five more in graduate school, school-weary Archbishop had been struggling as a daytime fertilizer salesman in Hamilton City and working evenings as a tutor for SNMBWCC. He began teaching part-time, a class or two a semester, and then obtained a full-time position when the college opened a store-front operation in Columbus. That was when his "academic" life began–back in 1987.

He wanted to teach at a place like Hamilton State University, but he enjoyed his paycheck and good benefits at SNMBWCC.

Still, sometimes Archbishop wondered how his passion for Shelley and Wordsworth and Whitman got him involved in teaching ENG composition at a community college. He had always been interested in making spiritual sense of the natural world–and he had found, of all the literary work he had studied to date, Walt Whitman's catalogs of animals and botanical forms in *Song of Myself* to be most relevant to his own world view. His dissertation study, "Hidden Angels in Whitman's *Leaves of Grass*," was mightily unrelated to teaching writing in comp classes. But he wasn't complaining. Maybe just surprised his career morphed into writing instruction rather than literary analysis.

There were some attributes of the university life he did not miss. Not a bit. Archbishop would admit he had always promoted good writing skills (punctuation, spelling, paragraphs) rather than political empowerment. At SNMBWCC, he frequently told his students his job was to help them write clearly, not further his or their political agendas. He tried to be a technician of sorts. Sort of a words and grammar mechanic.

Increasingly, though, he really became fixated with trying to figure out how he ended up teaching at a community college. Where had he gone wrong? He appreciated the tenets of community college ideology, but the culture seemed foreign to him. What had happened? Why couldn't he land a four-year school job despite hundreds of applications?

His dissertation committee had been composed of some stellar folks–national figures in their areas of expertise. He had published several articles about 19th century American romanticism and transcendentalism.

2

But there was always been something missing in his personality, in his presence, in his Weltanschauung, which had kept him in his place. When he looked at his life and habits, he could sense what went wrong.

He didn't exude star power. He didn't command the attention of the room. He wasn't self-promoting. The blue-collar types on the Miller High Life commercials (flowers in a beer bottle, spit-shined janitor shoes) reminded him of him. Sort of. Such a man (or woman) knew the job at hand and worked hard. Like recently wealthy industrialists in a W.D. Howells' novel, Joe was not comfortable with his station. He realized he didn't dress well. Archbishop couldn't talk about wine.

And almost sacrilegiously, Archbishop couldn't imagine spending good money on a cruise or bus tour of Italy.

The world he lived and worked in seemed increasingly crazy to him. And this was the real issue. How can equality and diversity exist simultaneously? And be "celebrated" every half-minute? In the 4th dimension? Conflicted paradoxes, if he thought about such matters.

Truth of the matter was, he would rather be working on a motorcycle than sitting at a meeting discussing student success or feedback loops or faculty salaries. "Whitman–good. Motorcycles–good. Teaching at the community college? Well, I enjoy my students and colleagues. I'm not complaining," mused Archbishop out loud to himself. "But what is it? What is my problem?"

"At least I didn't go crazy like Jack Frost—or become a tyrant like Phil Dolly!"

(Something was not right with Dr. Archbishop. Or perhaps everything was right!)

Johnny Sparks, Welder

@ Vanguard Community College

Johnny Sparks heard about "going to college" almost daily during grades K-12. Young Johnny grew up in a family of lawyers. His mom and dad are a married "law team." They hoped the boy would get good grades in high school, so he could (at least) get a scholarship to a Big Ten university and then go to a prestigious law school and become a barrister and future partner in their family firm.

Didn't happen. Johnny saw and heard enough about attorneys on TV commercials, cable news, and the dinner table. Not for him.

But Johnny did go to college. And he loved it. He enrolled in the welding program at Copperfield Community, got his pipe welding certification, and now, at age twenty, makes 70K per annum in the fracking fields of North Dakota. He drives a new Dodge Hemi 4X4 truck and enjoys fishing and hunting. He no longer watches the crazy people on cable news, and he feels great pity for those ensnared by the artifice of opinions, victimization, and unrequited political analysis. He makes a living as a skilled tradesman and loves the open sky country of North Dakota. And his folks are very proud of him because he followed his dream.

Adam Bliss, Groundskeeper

@ Moonbucks Patio, Santa Rey, North New Mexico

Adam Bliss sat on a bar stool and watched the cold, dreary, late autumn rain drip pitifully off the corrugated patio cover. He noticed his Yamaha, a 1969 DT-1 Enduro, was staying dry under the tree where he'd parked it. The old but clean motorcycle looked oddly misplaced in time, almost baleful, in the mists. Tonight's crowd was thin on this creaky Moonbucks porch here in Santa Rey

Most of the patrons sat, isolated, completely inside the building, eyes glued to laptop screens or smart phones. Bliss was here tonight, like the last three Friday nights, to provide background guitar music for the gathered coffee snobs. Moonbucks' corporate policy forbade payment to musicians, but he would be given free coffee and cakes for the following week (as payment in kind.) But not even a gift card, he considered wryly.

He usually made six or seven dollars from tips—and he kept a nice clean gallon pickle jar nearby for that purpose.

Bliss had been working at the community college over in Hamilton City as a groundskeeper for a couple of years. Married (for now anyway), he and his wife had a difficult, stormy relationship. He was a minimum wage college employee, and part-time musician, and she worked as a part-time carry-out at the Slipway Grocery Store.

Lately they had been fighting because of her new tattoos.

When romance became displaced by snacks and cooking shows blaring away 24/7 in his bedroom, he expressed concern. When he caught her making out with a city water meter reader, he'd had enough.

So, about three weeks ago, he left her in their apartment in Hamilton City and hauled himself over here to Santa Rey. Adam Bliss was now living in a run-down forty-five-year-old travel trailer in an RV park on a low hill by the river, just off Edison Avenue. The trailer had heat, running water, and a shower. Sometimes the roof leaked during a rain storm. He had worked out a deal with management—he'd function as the on-site "go to guy" and do minor fixes and repairs for the other fifty-one residents of this five-bar resort. In return, his rent was a nominal one hundred dollars monthly. So, after his 180 mile commute to Hamilton City for his college job each day in his diesel 4 X 4, he did a few repairs around the RV Park. It wasn't too bad. Sometimes he had quite a bit to do on the weekends, but he managed to keep Fridays open.

He was using this weekly Moonbucks gig as a way, he thought, to hopefully advertise himself as a musician. He knew something good was just ahead, just waiting to happen. He couldn't sing worth a lick, but he could play guitar and bass pretty well.

So tonight, he was getting ready to play, eyeing the empty tip jar, and hoping for a good show.

Suddenly, his dream of dreams, his fantasy lady, forcefully walked in, wearing Capris pants, hair ribbons, pale lipstick, and hoop earnings. And knee-high boots. What a looker!

Her new pearl necklace and wedding ring sparkled first-class, and his feelings at this moment reminded old Bliss of those emotions he once endured when a beautiful girl caught his eye in a club or at the horse track.

Wow. She sat down with three other well-heeled gals and ordered a glass of water and a chocolate muffin. They launched into a discussion of vampire novels, *Fixer Upper* episodes, gossip, and the next church social. He thought she might be a recently-hired full-time Professor of Biology at the college, but he wasn't sure. Wow.

Regaining his composure, Bliss busied himself tuning his guitar, which was rapidly going sharp in the damp air.

But his eyes were fixed on her curves, her presence, and her chattiness. And she was thin.

Now Bliss had been emotionally beaten, many times, under the roof of his former rent-by-the-week domicile. His manly wife had set him straight on most issues–especially on how couples should behave in public and in private. His wife had always been impressed by windbags, hard drinkers, and gnarly old dudes with white beards.

He wanted so badly to have romantic feelings, to write love songs, to bring flowers, to feel the throb and pulse of fulfilled love, and the gentle touch of a woman's willing lips.

So–Adam Bliss, in an emotionally fragile state, nearly broke, sort of on the lam, tired, and psychologically beaten, had been smitten instantly by a beautiful, shapely, nicely-dressed, and clearly-married woman. What would he do?

Well.

He sat on the stool and caught snatches of their conversation. He was trying to glean some significance, some meaning, some clue, for why their paths were crossing.

Not much came through.

Finally, in the key of G (his best vocal slot), Adam Bliss broke into an original song, strumming his slightly amplified Rickenbacker 330 in the dim glow of the three LED stage lights. He knew this song had great power. Trembling, and synthetically powered by his semi-hollow body guitar, he began to sing carefully:

Are you waiting there for me–?
while the light breaks from my Rickenbacker?
Are you thinking bits of me–?
making my life tick a little faster?
Are you dreaming? Are you mine?
Can you help my places grow and nourish?
Did you drive those miles for me?
And never sleep a wink 'cause
We were loving...
Did you wander to the sea–taking photos of the sunsets flooding?
Are you certain of your heart–and the life ahead you think of starting?
Tender moments come from always parting...
Can't we be, just what we are?
Two fates a-pounding on this middle-class star
Can't we be, just what we seem?
Afraid of nothing but the happiness dream?

While he was beginning the last chorus, the four women noisily got up and left without looking at him. They also ignored the tip jar on the way out. Bliss was still admiring her scientific curves as she walked off the patio into the misty night, pointing at his motorcycle, and laughing hysterically at any fool who would ride in the rain.

(Based on a storyline from *Love in the RV Park*, Rogue Phoenix Press, 2013 by Jeffrey Ross)

Dr. Brown Quits His Job

@ East Omaha Community College

Dr. August Brown drove out of the East Omaha Community College staff parking lot carefully. His car tires crunched over some frozen chunks of snow left by the last-named winter storm. As late as last week, he had been thinking about trading in his 1996 Corolla on a newer model.

Brown was attached to the car in a funny way—he really couldn't let go of the relationship with the Toyota—like many of the connections in his somber life that kept going on and on because they had some sort of abject functional value. He had nursed the car back to life so many times. It looked rough, but still ran. And the heater worked.

But he wouldn't be able to buy a new car for a while.

He had quit his job just this morning. He hadn't really planned on it, but something finally snapped. Mocked. Neglected. Desecrated. The switch had flipped. Work at that crazy community college meant nothing to him.

He couldn't be sure if his boss, Dean Preston Paxson, was yet aware he had quit. The Dean was away at a Higher-Learned Conference. The two hadn't spoken for months anyway. Come to think of it, he wasn't sure anybody knew he had quit.

He had simply typed a note, "Is this all you got? I quit. Dr. Brown," left it on Dean Paxon's desk, and vacated the building catacombs. His career as an HR specialist was apparently over.

Brown hadn't bothered to take any of his personal possessions—the mournful detritus of his sad, bill-paying working life was flippantly left behind.

Dr. Brown had conveniently abandoned his e-cigarette charger and faux smokes—left them still emitting cool, artificial vapor in the office. He would buy a pack of non-filtered Camels again. Probably later tonight or tomorrow. Now he anticipated the hopeful and endearing buzz of nicotine—and the whitish aroma of fragrant but paper-charring tobacco smokes. Was smoking going to kill him at his age? What difference did it make? He hungered for a non-filtered smoke! Bad!

Brown wondered what was better—quitting his job or not having to carry anything out of the office. He assumed the boss would be angry, his coworkers perplexed. Or not. (Later, each swore they were glad to see him go. Finally.)

He had been driving around town for hours, just roaming around, rolling to wherever, running some stop signs but hurting no one.

The journey to nowhere was cathartic. Easing. Pleasing.

Finally, he was reenergized. He found his way to the Copper Coin Saloon and a stool at the bar. Gazing at the hundreds of iconic pennies under the plexiglass countertop and slowing drinking a twenty-five-ounce super-chilled Blitz draft beer, he felt redeemed.

Speaking to himself in the big mirror hanging behind the bar (and peering over whiskey bottles so he could make eye contact!) he said out loud, "I can't believe I lasted twelve years at the college. All those meetings and pretentious people. Don't they realize they are owned and manipulated by the testing services and software? I really don't want to complain—I'm sure they are all happy working there. But how can those guys wearing suits and ties have jobs, good jobs, talking about something which doesn't matter once they leave the campus? I don't want to be negative. I just don't need such a job to be fulfilled or happy."

"The truth of the matter is I'd rather work as a cook in a fast food restaurant than trade my soul for a pretend life. I worked at a high school for a few years back in the day and thought that was tough, but nothing can top East Omaha Community. The language of learning has been replaced by buzzing—the endless distillations of teamwork, succession planning, and emails. I'm not lazy or nuts; I just can't be an actor anymore. I want to be happy, and I want to live a decent and fulfilling life and maybe contribute in a real or meaningful way. Doesn't anyone realize we still live analog lives?"

"I just don't fit in with that world. Maybe I've outgrown that place. Or perhaps it is tired of me too."

Brown ordered another Big Beer. He would apply for a job at a hardware or auto parts store tomorrow. And be helpful again. Gazing at his remaining beer, he wondered if hardware store employees had to attend meetings daily. "Hmm. Landscaping might be a better option," he mumbled out loud to no one.

(Based on a storyline from *The Auroran: Cold Front Redemption* Rogue Phoenix Press, 2015) by Jeffrey Ross)

Kat Van Dorn, Professor of English

@ Copperfield Community College

Professor Van Dorn is feeling pretty good about herself. In her second year of teaching at Copperfield, Kat is recognized as a strong faculty member, a good committee team player, and an active participant in community events. She received her Master's in Rhetoric and Composition from Hamilton State University three years ago, graduating cum laude and confident. While at HSU as a graduate student and full-time instructor, she served as an editor of the college's Literary Journal, helped organize their annual international conference on writing, and published several articles in national peer-reviewed journals including *The English Journal, College Composition and Communications, The Rhetorical Quarterly, and Feminism Today.*

At thirty, her teaching experiences are rich. She has taught on Interactive Television, online using both Web CT and Blackboard course management systems, and in traditional face-to-face situations. When eligible for a sabbatical in five more years, she hopes to complete her dissertation in Rhetoric and Composition at the University of Hamilton, located in Santa Rey, eighty-nine miles to the south.

Kat had concerns about "pausing" in her academic career to teach at a community college. But several considerations influenced her decision to apply for the then-open position at Copperfield. She knew that a stint of teaching in the community college classroom, working with emerging and developing writers, would give her experiences that could not be duplicated in the university–either as student or instructor.

Plus, as a committed academic professional, she knew very well that teaching writing at any level can be rewarding, helpful, and contribute to her knowledge base about methods, activities, and internal and external classroom learning processes.

Finally–she needed a job–and the community college full-time position paid far better (three times as much!) than what she could receive as a master's level instructor at Hamilton State U.

Her university colleagues had warned her about the teaching/

learning environment at the community college–and she had received many good-natured jabs from them following the interim President's DUI arrest.

Still, she was convinced her work was important at Copperfield–and her vision, purpose, and intellect were clear and focused...

"Kat," her doctoral advisor and long-term friend Dr. Haller from U of H said to her three years ago, "I hope you are making the right decision to take the position at CCC. I know the pay is attractive, but you will be spending much of your time involved in non-academic activities at CCC. There will be many days when you feel like a cashier at Sticky Mart–and you may be treated like one, too. Please, please don't desert your dissertation.

Be careful your pedagogic and academic sensibilities do not, uh, change too much. Protect, my dear, what Matthew Arnold would call your 'buried life.' Please, be brave, my child," she said, tears welling up in her eyes. (Dr. Haller turned away, wiping her eyes, then embraced Kat and wished her well, wished her the best.)

This reaction, and advice, had startled Kat momentarily, but she did not allow Dr. Haller to dissuade her from her decision–nor had she allowed her ensuing time at CCC to modify her behaviors, interests, or academic endeavors.

During the past three years, she had maintained a detached, objectivist, clinical eye on her surroundings.

Old Doc Roz, bearded friend, would-be poet, and grandfatherly confidant, Chair of the Rhetoric Division at HSU, had benignly sent her one of the articles he had published years ago about community colleges and middle-class values.

"Read this, my dear. You may find it enlightening as you descend into the maelstrom of community college life! Somehow you must prepare for the intellectual erosion, the whimsical culture that awaits you!

Kat smiled, remembering that moment, and considered how the old man's academic career had been built on Op-Eds and newsletter articles. But, she thought, at least he wrote... And, he apparently wrote some gangbuster pieces back in 2007 or 2008–but not much of merit since then.

Well, not that this new non-academic life was perfect. She was uncomfortable with the Professor title given master's level teachers at

Copperfield–even though she had a significant publication and presentation record.

(Strange, she marveled. At Copperfield we have a Professor of Plumbing and two Professors of Custodial Science. I wonder if they have written scholarly articles about soldering flux, Teflon tape, or broom handle durability.)

She was amazed at how much energy the faculty at Copperfield spent on meetings–daily meetings about quality initiatives, constituency labor concerns, salary negotiations, golf tournaments, strategic planning, organizational learning, wellness exams, potlucks, and even baby showers.

Kat reckoned she spent sixty percent of her on campus time at college restructuring and reorganization meetings.

"There is so much talk about critical thinking among the faculty," she whispered to herself, "but it is much like an advertising campaign, or ideas for a web page...I wonder how many of the faculty members truly understand the liberating nature, the egalitarian qualities, of a great books curriculum or the liberal arts?"

Coming from an intensive and fruitful academic environment at a Research I University, she was often overwhelmed and obfuscated by the stress and anxiety evidenced by the CCC faculty in terms of their teaching loads, overload pay schedules, and office size.

They acted so much like "labor," she found herself thinking more than once. *Or like young-uns!*

The daily dose of management meetings, quality initiatives, and outcomes assessment usually seemed far removed from her students' actual learning needs.

While she would never voice her feelings publicly–or in the faculty lounge or hallways or offices like so many of her colleagues at Copperfield–she had many questions about the actual competency and intentions of the administrators, especially the President and Dean Preston. *Pleasant enough men, they talked incessantly, but in actuality did so little,* she thought to herself. She often marveled at the proliferation of dean and vice president positions the last few months at CCC–and she wondered what many of these people would do–or how they would be perceived–at a major university such as HSU.

(She heard, in her mind, old man Roz laughing again–"Ha Ha!")

Why did all of these administrators hold or seek a doctorate in leadership? Why was the Ed Leadership doctorate a necessary "union card" for entry into an upper level "leadership" role in the American community college?

Based on the age-old academic model she understood, university administrators came out of academic departments–beginning their careers in academia as educational experts, seeking the terminal degree became an essential pathway to knowledge acquisition. They were academicians and scholars (teachers) in a subject matter discipline who earned entry into higher education based, almost entirely, on their academic insight and discipline expertise.

Grounded in the principles required for scientific inquiry and truth finding, these professionals thrived because they knew "something." They had a thorough understanding of subject matter–scientific methodological approaches–based on theoretical models or frameworks and experimental practice. Having intellectual depth and understanding of theory frames used in inquiry, they also possessed a deep comprehension of complex organizational approaches to problem solving and arriving at a measurable level of truth.

She knew the most successful demonstration of leadership can be seen in any number of history's prized leaders. Included were those in the military, in politics, in business, and in religious orders. True leaders – Soldiers, Generals, Princesses, Kings, Queens, Senators, Judges, Presidents, Governors, Mayors, CEO's CFO's, Ministers, Priests, Rabbis, Bishops, Popes–well, their leadership success did not require doctoral coursework, degree accomplishment, credentials, self-centered networking, or weekend seminars at a golf resort...

Was it possible for paper work to provide leadership?

Why was the non-academic doctorate apparently a requirement for community college "leaders"?

She was baffled sometimes by the posturing, the posing, and the corporate nomenclature surrounding, simply engulfing, daily discourse at CCC. The alleged "myths" and "misplaced" and "inappropriate" stereotypes of community college culture she had heard about on the "outside" seemed painfully, and sadly, accurate now that she was an employee. "I will never go native," she whispered to herself, after a painful reorganization meeting–at which Dr. Dolly huffed and puffed about higher education leadership. (She knew Dolly had written nothing–except for clandestine and probably accusatory notes in his ever-present journal–presented nowhere, and had been fired from his last job...)

She daily found the administrative team naïve in their understanding of complex issues–and they often used words, almost like junior high kids, at the periphery of their knowledge base. She considered composing an article discussing the role p laying, the scripted behaviors she found among community college administrators. But who would publish such a thing? And who would read it? These people want to hear success stories, not criticism. I wonder if they ever read anything–or write anything. They are experts at copying and pasting, and recommending someone to "take the lead" on projects! And they always seem so defensive. She was simply amazed that so little community college criticism or reform literature had ever been produced.

Anthropologists would be stunned if they conducted an honest, scholarly ethnographic study of this place! Copperfield Community culture was so insular, so protected, so, uh grades 13-14.

"Property taxes," once quipped gruff Doc Roz while he stroked his Walt Whitman beard. "That's all that keeps 'em solvent," he said, as he walked off to light his meerschaum pipe." (Another memory–she could still smell his Captain Bleak tobacco as he wandered down the literature building hallway...) "Remember, my dear, in America everything is the opposite of how it seems to be!"

Still, Kat loved her students–loved teaching. She was highly respected and had a tremendous work ethic. She was quick to lead when called and exhibited the highest levels of professionalism. She was an old-time professor–dedicated to her discipline and the academic life. In some ways, at the young age of thirty, she felt overly mature, overly serious, in the daily circus of Copperfield Community.

She had learned to grow silent and contemplative at meetings, but to volunteer to "take the lead" on writing or research projects. At HSU, as an instructor, her committee work had been focused on academic activities.

At CCC, the committees seemed to be focused on responding to threats or warding of threats–external or internal, real or imagined.

Her academic weltanschauung had thus far preserved her from embracing the apparent foibles of Copperfield culture.

Kat was surprised to learn few faculty members ever applied for grants–and still fewer tried to publish articles or even Op-Eds. "I'm here to teach. I'm not interested in that publish or perish mentality," she overheard Dr. S. Chick say at a department meeting. She knew many had made "best practices" presentations at local conferences or regional community college conferences–and they were to be commended for this–but she was surprised that so little scholarly work was produced–or attempted–at CCC.

She had also discovered seventy percent of the CCC Professorship held the MA as their highest degree, but only one besides herself was working on a PhD in an academic area. Fifty-four were in a cohort pursuing Ed. Leadership degrees from the University of Topeka, hopefully to prepare themselves for careers as Deans, VP's and ultimately Presidents (at CCC and beyond!). The union card for community college leaders!

Kat was pleased to learn she had won a BISON (Big Institute for Staff and Organized Normalization) award for teaching excellence, but her joy was tempered somewhat when she learned seventeen other CCC faculty members also received their BISON plaques. (Her happiness was further dampened when she received word from Dean Preston that there was travel money for BISON, but not for the National Combine of English Teachers national conference, where she was scheduled to make a presentation on embedded tutoring). In her usual even-tempered way, she simply murmured to herself, "Well, I've got a lot to learn about community college culture."

Kat sometimes wonders if the administrative staff–with their generous salaries and inflated egos–could grasp the irony of the school's name: Copperfield Community College. Dickens's novel, *David Copperfield,* she mused, was about class consciousness and the wide gulf between social classes in Victorian England. Well, she considered, we can certainly observe class distinctions at CCC! She wondered, also, how many faculty members or administrators in the district had ever read a Dickens novel—or even the local newspaper. Or their mail.

(Originally published in *College Leadership Crisis: The Philip Dolly Affair* Rogue Phoenix Press, 2011 by Jeffrey Ross and Jann M. Contento.)

Adjuncts in Love

@ Silver State Technical Community College

Mr. Frost did not appear troubled on the exterior. But inside, he was filled with churning emotions and agitations. One of his former (full-time) colleagues, the now-retired Prof. Richard Hose, M.A., described Jack, "He's like a duck—calm on the surface but paddling like h— underwater." Frost's poems, which his few (extremely few) readers would probably judge "fair to middling" in quality, revealed his uncanny ability to capture the great sadness, and few joys, in life's daily movements. Jack was increasingly an observer, not a participant.

Frost was a part-time Spanish instructor (without a future) at Silver State Technical Community College (SSTCC), home of the "Whoosh" mascot, in Hamilton City, West New Mexico. In Frost's mind (and experiences), life had dealt him one disappointment after another. He left a decent full-time grammar school teaching job to take on several part-time sections at the college—at the decision-point of his initial "hiring" at SSTCC, a since long-departed Dean (who is now a successful community college President somewhere in Eastern Wales) assured him he would have a good chance at becoming a full-timer in just a year or two. (That was in 1995. Twenty-four years have passed.)

Frost had been married twice—his first betrothal lasted five years and gave him six children (now all grown and alienated from their erratic and pato-like semi-professor father). Frost currently resides in a nice, though weather-beaten, 20 x 50 doublewide mobile home at the Hamilton Inn Mobile Home Park. Mr. Frost, who vowed never to marry again, now rooms with another adjunct, one Dr. Buzz "C. C." Blocker. (Sidebar: Dr. Buzz is bright but an iffy housekeeper, loves bowling, pubs and happy hours, has more credit debt than the US treasury, hobbles on bad knees, and is about worn out from her frustrations. Dr. Buzz is an Adjunct Professor of Reading/Biology/Sociology/GED Studies/Radiology at SSTCC.)

Together, if they both teach four classes during the semester, they take in about 15,000 dollars per annum. As they say, misery loves company. But Dr. Buzz, to her credit, does supplement her income with a part-time bar tending gig down at the Copper Coin Saloon. (And she makes a mean frozen margarita!) They are overtly unhappy, but together, the academic-minded couple makes enough money to pay rent and buy a few groceries (mostly canned goods and bourbon).

Hopelessly a romantic, Jack is compelled to write and dream big dreams, despite his daily confrontations with a thorny reality which include a lousy income and related life issues.

Frost rides a fully broken-in 1965 Honda 305 Dream motorcycle to work most of the time. Some days it is just too cold or icy. Then he rides his bicycle or Razor scooter. His faded yellow Del Yugo Moto sedan, paralyzed by a busted motor, sits on blocks in his front yard. Frost has been unable to find the money to fix the car the last six years, so the old four-banger lingers solemnly, just off the street, a rusting and mute testament to his financial condition–and the better, happier, suburban times he once enjoyed with wife number two (before she left him for a bug exterminator).

Jack Frost had significant plans earlier in life. He wanted a cabin in the forest. He hoped to obtain a PhD in Spanish literature, perhaps concentrating on Spanish subjective romanticism–most likely concerning the work of Mariano José de Larra (1890-1837–ironically a suicide because of a love affair gone bad!). But this accomplishment never came to pass. Shortly after his second marriage–while he was still teaching at Giltner Grammar School–he somehow hopped onto this adjunct treadmill at Silver State TCC. (Oh, those times, those feelings, those decisions were so complex and muddleheaded. What had he done? What was he thinking?)

He had wanted to be a college professor so badly! He thought he was leaving behind misbehaving students, senseless meetings, salary schedule dilemmas, misguided conference-and-career addicted administrators, politicized governing boards, and petty staff squabbles. Well. He still dealt with most of that litany of despair daily, made one fifth the money, and had no health insurance. Or a guaranteed parking spot at SSTCC (home of the "Whoosh" Mascot)!

Frost had been teaching six four-credit (but non-transfer) Conversational Spanish classes a year since 1995–and occasionally took eager monolingual senior citizens on tours of Juarez or Tijuana or El Golpho de Santa Clara. The carrot of a full-time teaching position–with bennies and good pay, and social prestige, still dangled deliciously in front of him. Year after year, he doggedly awaited the death or retirement of a full-time SSTCC faculty member (or their almost always pre-destined promotion to a deanship) for a slot to open. And then–but of course, department politics were strange–even stranger than at Gilbert Grammar back in the old prosperous days...

A realist, Frost continued to apply for full-time positions at more notable or interesting institutions. (He maintains a folder which currently contains one hundred ninety-three rejection notices.) He had recently interviewed at Northeastern Sussex West University and Illinois Southern North Central State Polytechnic. Absolutely nothing came from these efforts except further rejections. Private schools–land grant universities– directional colleges. Nope. Nobody wanted him.

A Division III college soccer player earlier in life, he had even applied for some assistant athletic director jobs. Nada.

To improve his prospects, Frost had been enrolled in an online University of Topeka-at Bangladesh cohort Ed. Leadership program for a while. The curriculum, great expense, chatty students, and endless menu-planning, drove him away quickly. He just didn't want to be an administrator or social networker.

He had neither the time, money, intellect, nor focus to enroll in a real academic PhD program at this point in his life. Besides, such an academic degree would mean nothing at SSTCC. (Oh-one of his friends from the local university, old Doc Arlo, admonished him: "Ach, a PhD is the kiss of death over there at Whoosh-Ville! Ya'd know too much, lad! Ach!") His savings were meager. He lived check to check. He had no idea where the money went. None.

He had forged a kind of baseline data efficiency approach to existence which allowed him to steam ahead–at the expense of many experiences, many opportunities.

Frost had few friends. He saw Professor of Humanities S. Chick, D. A., as an isolated, bizarre work-shirking anachronism. Old Chick wore "stuffy shirts" and carried around yellowing lecture notes. Frost once thought often about Julia Flowers–the lovely, red-headed, extremely bright adjunct Speech and Rhetoric Professor. Perhaps he still hoped for something, but he saw her now as someone out of touch and subsidized by a rich husband.

He occasionally had lunch with Dr. Bruce Martinez, but Frost was simply not interested in Marxist politics. Or intellectual diversity.

He had been a fair athlete in his day and had committed himself to a life time of physical fitness. While his jogging program had slowed, he still had the habit of maintaining the prisoners' workout regimen in the front yard whenever possible (using scattered free weights, jugs of ale, cinder blocks, 4 x 4 fence posts—whatever was available). He was lean and strong, but...he smoked and drank too much, too, though he had been told countless times he simply had to quit the cigarettes. (He had made so many resolutions to give up the Lucky Strikes!)

Recently, his thyroid had begun giving him trouble—his joints were wearing out—and small patches of skin cancer had been cut off his scalp. He took all of this to be a sign of fatalistic doom—further proof of the bad hand he had been dealt by fate and college administrators. He had no health or dental insurance and had not been "in" for a physical for decades. (And one of his back molars was screaming for extraction!)

Frost had a dreary, tasked commitment to his job. He was always available to help students after class. He received good reviews and did what was expected of him by the institution. He did not openly rant about politics on campus or gossip around the "water cooler." He had no retirement plan to review or nurture and no conferences to attend. Beaten up by reality and bad breaks repeatedly, he took no giddy pleasure in pep talks by administrators.

The community college provided a paycheck and a storyline ("Me? Oh, I teach at the college"). Yet, his proletarian efforts went largely unnoticed by students, staff, and even loving Professor Buzz.

The world of new cars and flat screen 5K TV's—well, it all seemed like some sort of life-script that he would never be able to afford. His quiet time reflections—few as they were—while walking through a flowery (in summer) wooded park or on the banks of a muddy stream—such moments seemed to have priceless value to him—immeasurable moments of poetic ecstasy that no one seemed to "get"—or even wished to acknowledge. The scripted economic circus flourishing around him simply debilitated him.

The 21st century buzzing hive of commoditized learning at his college both fascinated and discouraged him. Teaching and learning, he often considered, have been replaced by whimsical conversations about careers. I go to work and swim in a kind of philosophic compost quagmire, a sinkhole of self-service. Thoreau, thought Frost to himself, would certainly notice the many lives of "quite desperation" ploddingly manifested all around the campus.

He could not fathom how men like the new college President, Dr. Philip Fishinrico, and his supervising Dean, Dr. Paxton Preston, had such big salaries and impressive lake-front second homes. He wondered if they had ever learned a second language, or read poetry, or struggled to pay utility bills. How many FTSE did they produce? How many students did they know by name?

(Sidebar: Frost really liked the President's flirty secretary, Rebecca. He wondered if she made most of the BIG decisions around campus.)

At sixty Jack hadn't known a lot of happiness. He was a locust–still buzzing, but a shell, a cicada husk stuck on a dried tree. The vampires had destroyed him. He taught his classes, tutored students, attended a division meeting now and then, struggled to find a place to park his Razor scooter, and went home to blissful Buzz.

Frost had many issues, many lingering and malingering emotional concerns. Sometimes at night, he would awaken and see figures in his room. The phantasms were always different. For example, one night he saw Dr. Fishinrico, sweating and cursing, painfully bent over and mowing the lawn up at his six-story lakefront cabin. Once he even saw Obama and Richard II playing tennis together in Alaska while Sarah Palin stirred lemonade in the distance.

What did Frost want? Well, Frost wanted to be heard at department meetings–he wanted an office (a cubicle would do) at the college–he wanted the key code to a copier–he wanted access to a computer in a private place, somewhere away from students and the giggling, noisy library staff– he wanted more than $1750 a semester for teaching a four-credit hour class–but most of all, he wanted some respect. And benefits. (That tooth was really hurting). Oh, and he needed a place to keep his Razor scooter while he was in class.

Adjunct Be Not Loud

A poem by Prof. Jack Frost

(With special thanks to John Donne)

(Rejected by twenty-six journals and blogs, but happily discovered in a waste basket by a pretentious and literary custodian.)

@ Silver State Technical Community College, Room F134

Adjunct, be not loud, though exploited be.
Willing and happy, for thou have no place;
With those who make thee teach in largest space
Filled not by timers full, for nearly free.
No decent wage, nor wholesome healthcare perk
Nor parking; where does joy of teaching go?
What academic galley must ye row?
To pay back loans, and in the taverns lurk.
Thou art slave to books, and cold admin's ire
And dost with brown bag jelly sandwich dwell,
And thermos'd coffee makes you teach as well.
D—d quirky fate, no job app to aspire?
One dean gets a raise or corporate turns,
And Adjunct works no more; Adjunct shalt "retire."

Henry Mc Dougal, Second Shift Socialist Barkeep

@ The Copper Coin Saloon

Mc Dougal was a tough character. In the dead of the North New Mexico winter, he could be seen wearing a tank top, shorts, and heavy snow boots, puffing on a pipe, a red wool beret tipped to one side of his bald head. He has an anchor tattooed on one arm and his family coat of arms on the other.

Few of the patrons in the bar know he was formerly Comrade "Fightin' Boy" Mc Dougal of the North Scotland Militant Socialist Movement (NSMSM), a violent social reformer who got his kicks fighting Capitalists at football matches and who marched in Glasgow every May 1. He was known as a bit of an enforcer–he loved to smash heads and property, and he was also adept at writing scathing anti-capitalist articles in the local socialist newspaper.

He keeps a duffle bag filled with ball bats, brass knuckles, machetes–the tools of his trade–in case he is called upon again...

Ach, those were the good old days. I miss those dear times with me friends and colleagues. We really had a chance to show them exploiters what we wuz made of, he thought to himself. But things got a little too hot for him in Glasgow–he had heard MI Five or Scotland Yard or somebody was looking for him on a murder warrant *(I had nothin' to do with tha' Irishman, tha' mad rocket, for sure–ach, but they wuz huntin' me down like The Big Grey Man of Ben MacDhui!),* so he left his wife (and six kids) a farewell letter and caught a steamer to Ellis Island.

After kicking around in New York (then mostly neglected by soft and overfed American Socialists), he decided to give the West a try–and his in-depth knowledge of Scotch whisky, ale, and his big arms, helped him land a job at the Copper Coin (eventually). He was initially hired on as a bouncer, working when the Coin hosted live bands, but he finally moved up the working ranks and now he slung whisky and beer for a living.

Now, Mc Dougal was an educated man–he had taken a Degree in Economics at the University of Stirling–though it took him six or seven years because of small-offense jail terms. He was well acquainted with the ways of university faculty members and principals. But this lot from the local college was just amazing to him. They didn't tip *"worth a dom,"* but he heard they made all kinds of money; they crept around like criminals, and generally came across as a bunch of bampots! (Scottish vernacular for confused people.)

They didn't want to talk about football or even American sports– they were always looking for donations, trying to get him to sign partnership agreements, and giving him advice about how he should become a life-long learner.

Ach, they always whine about being offended, networking and pathways, and their d—d cell phones apps, and their goofy packaged tours abroad! What the h—! They wouldn't know what good socialism was if it ran over 'em like a Venezuelan locomotive! AOC? Pah! Another pretender!"

He had tried to start a Socialist Students' Union group on the CCC campus, but those *"d—d Capitalist exploiters"* in charge of the college would hear nothing of such a student group...

Many of 'em wouldn't even buy a belly washer but would sit at the bar with a glass of water ('with lemon and a straw, please') and try to sell him raffle tickets, recipe books, or advertising space in the college catalog. (He did once buy a city discount coupon book from some adjunct faculty member and found the online dating advertising section interesting. *Ach!*) None of the CCC people seemed particularly bright–he tried to talk to one Dean or Principal about Hegel, trying to strike up an interesting conversation one afternoon when the bar was near empty, but the poor fellow was thinking he said bagels and asked if the Copper Coin had any cream cheese."

"Ach," exclaimed McDougal. "I think I'll move to California where there be real socialists!"

(Originally published in *College Leadership Crisis: The Philip Dolly Affair* (Rogue Phoenix Press, 2011) by Jeffrey Ross and Jann M. Contento)

Experimental College Residence Life Project Burns to Ground!

@ East Mesa Community College

East Mesa Community College saw its recent North New Mexico property acquisition burn to the ground last week.

EMCC had purchased the iconic sixty-five-year-old Hamilton County RV Park last April for sixteen-million dollars, amidst controversies about the property's actual value and the well-being of long-term RV Park residents.

EMCC's residence staff had planned to use the trailers for temporary overflow student housing and to celebrate transient habitat-specific cultural diversity.

Newly-homeless park residents were angry with the college.

Tensions had been growing between EMCC and the RV residents, who were evicted to make room for EMCC students. Former park residents had organized several protests and a sit-in at the college's Staten Administration Building.

A spokesman for victim-residents, Mr. Sol Davies, believes the college "intentionally started the fire to intimidate senior citizens who lived in the RV park. EMCC wanted us old-timers out and probably thought burning down some trailers would speed up the process. But the fire went crazy. Morons!"

No injuries were reported in the overnight five-alarm blaze, although thirty-three trailers and motorhomes were destroyed, along with a National Historic Registry-listed cinder block recreation hall and the park's laundry building, which housed two twenty-five cents-a-load avocado-themed washing machines and a Teem pop machine.

Fire Chief Terry Booker suspects arson, but no arrests have been made. "We have no leads, but several whacky characters live in the park, and even more work at the college."

East Mesa Community College President Philip Jenkins, concerned about EMCC's image following the displacement of park residents, hopes to bring healing to Hamilton City.

27

"We are very distressed," said Jenkins. "Certainly, our institution played no part in this unfortunate event. EMCC has been a smoke-free campus for a year. Matches and lighters have been prohibited on campus. One of the RV park residents may have ignited the place by carelessly smoking tobacco or medicinal marijuana.

"Let the healing process begin," added Jenkins. "Our prayers go out to those park residents who have lost homes and livelihoods. Yet, in some small way, as we begin the rebuilding process, perhaps social justice has been served!"

Jenkins has called for a complete investigation by local, state and federal agencies.

"We are one East Mesa, one Mesa, one RV park–a diverse but vibrant community committed to a focused mission and a strategic plan. We stand in solidarity with the displaced and victimized residents. Yass! We are one big family, and families go through trying times. In a 21st century filled with challenges and opportunities; our partnerships must be nourished by a commitment to provide inexpensive yet sustainable housing for students."

Jenkins indicated he would assign EMCC staff to help the former park residents reassess personal goals for their future lives and life-long learning activities.

Counselor Celina Durango will take the lead in this rebuilding process, which Jenkins hopes will become a "sustainable partnership with those diverse community stakeholders who have recently joined the homeless community and who find themselves displaced by the fire."

Jenkins further indicated EMCC has opened the college's gymnasium to forty-two now-homeless former RV Park residents. EMCC will provide cots for sleeping and two ravioli-flavored Meals-Ready-To-Eat twice a day.

Wilhelm Brown, the college's public information director, said the former park residents would be asked to leave the gym when EMCC begins classes next week.

(Adapted from a Jeffrey Ross story originally printed on the *Cronk News* website)

Professor Jack Frost Comes Home

@The 300 Road near Happy Jack, Arizona

Jack Frost comes home from his teaching job...
Numb from the cold, he
struggles to get a crinkled key into the front door (frozen fingers, you know).

He is living in an older travel trailer now, just off a numbered forest road–

Alimony, bad health, and depression have pretty much cleaned him out.

He doesn't pay attention to scrolling marquees or television...the icons of pop culture are so just so much debris to Frost...

.

The World has beaten him badly–perhaps his fault, perhaps not...
He has a job and pays his bills and, he sees silliness in society
Old Professor Frost treats himself to smoked oysters and a six pack of good cold beer each Friday night...

He has no photographs in his place, nor phones, nor any past or future... Just the present...

And his memories focus and refocus on those who have ridiculed him mercilessly...

He doesn't go to movies or stream music (he owns an AM radio, but not a TV!)

(He reads and reflects quietly.)

You see–Jack Frost took that sage advice to be an individual–
"Never conform! Be yourself, do what you want to do! Just Be Happy!"

And the World has beaten him for it...
The World has beaten him badly–perhaps his fault, perhaps not–

Submission Rejection Delirium

At Gabbert General Hospital ER

Two ER physicians at Gabbert General Hospital in Gabbert, Arizona, huddled over the patient still strapped to a gurney. The white male, approximately Medicare age, had been brought in by ambulance just a few minutes earlier. He was unkempt, disheveled, and clearly in a distressed state. There were no signs of injury or trauma, and his vital signs were good, except for somewhat elevated BP. He had no ID, but he clutched a tattered, short manuscript in his left hand–authored by a Dr. Derik Hall. As he was also wearing a ring on his pinkie finger with the same initials "D. H." engraved inside the band, the attending staff assumed he was indeed Dr. Hall.

Also, the ER Team got a clue to his identity form his incoherent utterances. He kept mumbling or muttering something like "Vocational ed will save us from the barbarians," and "Please God not another meeting," and "No no no–not another rejection!"

Dr. Martin, the attending physician, asked objectively, "Any patient background information?"

Dr. Forrester, the resident who helped paramedics wheel Hall in the exam room, replied tersely: "He was seen wandering in an alley behind Dave and Brewster's Arcade down at the mall on Greenfield. Someone called 911 and paramedics were sent immediately. By the time they arrived, he was flat on his back in a puddle making snow-angel motions. They reported he was mumbling something about how all the publication houses were closing now' and that he had 'killed them-killed all of them.' The paramedic crew contacted Gabbert PD about a possible crime, but the authorities had no information about publication house murders, so the matter was dismissed. One of the paramedics told me the patient seemed quite delusional–a threat to both himself and society–so they picked him up and brought him here."

Dr. Martin seemed mildly concerned. He knew these academic cases were edgy, odd, fuzzy. "Well, I don't know. Start a standard hydration IV, run a blood gas panel, and see if you can contact any of his relatives. Maybe there is a clue to his residence or contact information in the sheets of paper he is holding. Let me pry...them...out of...those...fingers."

(Even in his semi-conscious state, Dr. Hall resisted the manuscript's departure–but he finally acquiesced.)

Martin, relieved, smoothed out the damp and muddy documents, sat down, and began reading. The paper is reprinted in its entirety below (in the interest of medical and psychological accuracy). Much of the text was mottled by brown water–and the edges were frayed and torn. But Martin quickly read the op-ed.

Practical Higher Education: Fostering Sustainable Student Workforce Skills Beyond the Academy
By Derik Hall, EdD, Adjunct English Faculty, Southern Arizona College

The Big Problem

Higher Education has created an increasingly recognizable subculture: The Broke and Underemployed. Many recent college graduates, especially those studying the liberal arts, have large amounts of debt and are frequently unprepared for entry into the American work-force.

Perhaps the American social fixation with Higher Ed ultimately contributes to the so-called wage gap–rather than to improve the economic situation of the American middle class. Too many people get degrees that don't get them jobs.

A Solution

My institution, like many other American community colleges, offers valuable applied science degrees to students. Briefly, for those of you who need a little "training," the AAS is a vocation-specific degree. A student seeking an AAS in Welding at my school will take forty-two credit hours of dedicated welding and technology courses. The degree also has a ten to twenty-three credit hour academic requirement of traditional courses in social sciences, math, English, and communications. (The remaining credit hours are in computer competency, professional, and business-related classes.)

Yes, job training degrees at community colleges require an academic component.

Consider the "opposite." What if all academic degrees required a job training component? Why not require all AA and BA degree recipients to take eighteen or so hours of job training course work—enough courses to earn a certificate or minor credential in medical transcription, culinary arts, or some other job-ready field?

Graduates of such programs might find work, real work. Such occupations could support students while they complete their undergraduate careers, and finance them through graduate school, or med school, and maybe, just maybe, help many discover a professional pathway. Visualize the tangible results: Nonfictional diversity within degree plans! Measurable competencies! Industry partnerships! Happy students!

Denouement

What if we stopped nourishing the self-fulfilling prophecy, the strange praxis of anger and victimization, by even partially reforming the culture of Higher Education? What if the secondary schools and the Department of Education stopped beating the drums for college readiness at the expense of specialized vocational skills? Let's support, rather than diminish the trades, the craftspeople, and knowledge too often perceived as non-academic.

Maybe we can best alleviate social injustice by helping our students more fully participate in a society that increasingly requires specific work-related skills and a decent, sustainable income. Mandating degree-seeking students to take a few job-skills courses as part of their academic programs will create a better "place" for all Americans...

Dr. Martin, hands trembling, dropped the paper to the floor. His eyes grew wide with recognition!

Dr. Martin was shocked. The silence was overpowering. Teetering as he stood up, he groaned. Then, a shriek. "What the h—-!" Good God. You should read this. He is tearing the very fabric of our democracy. Make college students study something that would help them get a regular old job? Everyone? Think of it! Me–a truck driver! The nerve!"

"That's it, Dr. Forrester. There is nothing we can do for him here. Have patient Hall transported to the psych ward over on Van Buren. He truly is a threat to American society! Where would anybody get such crazy ideas?"

Hall suddenly sat up and shouted, "When I submit, no one replies– or I learn the website gets shut down. I've killed them all! I've killed them all!"

Pandemonium broke out in the ER. Lights flashed, horns honked. Then, soothing opioids trickled down through Prof. Hall's IV–and he was calm once more. The health care professionals prepared Dr. Hall for his final submission.

Thinking outside the box has consequences.

Dr. Joy Lipton

@ Copperfield Community College.

Joy had been home-schooled. She was a child prodigy. Her mother, a former public-school educator, recognized Joy's abilities early, and left her teaching position to work with Joy. At age fourteen, Joy completed her high school diploma and enrolled at Copperfield Community College. The environment was perfect for her. She thrived at CCC. Dr. Roz was one of her professors. At age sixteen, she enrolled at the University of Southern Arizona and completed her bachelor's degree in two more years. By age twenty-two, she finished medical school and became a practicing M.D. Story just beginning. Community college can be a beautiful thing!

(Based on a true life narrative)

Residence Life Secretary Becomes President at West Mesa Community College

@ West Mesa Community College

This morning, governing board Member Adam Chess announced the hiring of an internal candidate to fill the long-vacant position of WMCC President.

"Yes," Chess told a group of gathered reporters outside the Hillary Clinton Communications Building, "we are quite pleased with our decision. The board has determined, after an extensive seven-month national search (costing taxpayers $6.4 million), one of our own long-time employees best fits the cultural and strategic needs of our diverse college community."

"We are pleased to announce Ms. Irma Kavanaugh, A.A.S, will assume the role of WMCC President effective January 1, 2015. Ms. Kavanaugh has served as the full-time Secretary of Residence Life at WMCC for eight years. Earlier, she served as Assistant Under-Secretary of Residence Life as a work-study student. She received both her G.E.D and A.A.S. degree from WMCC and is currently enrolled in an online BS in Management program at the University of Eastern Ajo–a respected online institution from southwestern Arizona and our higher education partner. She hopes to complete that program by Christmas. One of her exciting future goals is to teach management courses here as a successful adjunct faculty member! Yes, Irma Kavanaugh represents the best of our 'Grow our Young Uns' succession program!"

"We were looking for a multi-tasker, and we found one in Irma. Look. Everyone knows secretaries run schools. C'mon. If a dean or vice-president vanishes or doesn't come to work, no one would notice for a month or two. But if a division secretary goes missing, well–the college might collapse in a matter of hours."

"The external applicants we reviewed and interviewed seemed like so many career-driven clones. Their cover letters were written in nearly undecipherable corporate speak (filled with the usual references to mission statements, cultural change, leadership, critical thinking, social media, strategic plans, thundercloud-based course management systems, and Myway fundraisers). Boring!"

"Our external candidate pool, of course, represented exciting gender and cultural diversity, but not one of the multicultural-celebrating candidates had "It"–the elusive quality required of a successful CEO in today's higher education-leading, vibrant, transparent, quality-driven community colleges."

"None of the other interviewees said a thing about critical recipes, baby showers, bake sales, karaoke, dress-up days, dancing deans at fundraisers, coupons, or music downloads. In our view, Irma addressed all those learner-centered areas with confidence–she is a true leader."

"Most importantly, we noticed during the interview process that none of the other candidates stepped outside to take a personal call, checked their smartphones for text messages or videos, or burst out laughing inappropriately after viewing a meme. Such clearly professional behavior is an obvious problem, since every member of the WMCC staff, faculty, and student population spends about ninety percent of their "workdays" fixated on a tablet or smart phone, and frequently interrupts the learning environment with rude outbursts. Irma has that special connection with the WMCC family. She is one of us and understands our culture."

Chess further explained, "The Board was genuinely inspired when viewing a security camera video which captured and archived Irma's work habits and customer service skills. Members watched in warm amazement as Irma texted on her smart phone, played solitaire on her computer, ate pizza, cut her toenails, and laughed with partying students–simultaneously! Irma is engaged with our learners, our technology, and our stakeholders. She represents the best of the 21st Century and the future of our great learner-centered nation! Irma, without a doubt, has 'It.'"

Chess turned away to re-enter the building, and then concluded his remarks with a friendly wave. "Plus, she agreed to work for the same paltry president's salary of $660,000 per annum, and she agreed to not ask for a raise! Have a great day, everyone. I need to get back to my slice of quiche in the board room!"

(President-Select Irma Kavanaugh was unavailable for comment– she had reportedly taken a personal day to get a $15 Mani Pedi done in downtown Hamilton City. Sources indicate that she was pleased to hear about her new "easier" job but was now negotiating some kind of pay raise.)

(Adapted from a Jeffrey Ross story originally printed on the *Cronk News* website)

Professor Frost at the Birthday Party

@Gold Canyon, Arizona

Frost came down the still-chilled mountain to attend this warm-air birthday party.

He had hoped the band would let him sit in–he knew three or four chords.

But it didn't happen.

Now the tired party was just about tapped out. Bilingual Frost was sitting on a PA speaker,

sloshing down the last of a warming Bambi Bock beer, gazing across the patio at

a lovely dreadlock woman.

Same old Frost delusions–He was lonely, she was lonely, nothing would happen.

He was an outlier–didn't know the buzzwords, didn't spend more than he made, had

never watched American Idle (that's *Idol*, Frost!)–he belonged back up on the Rim, grading tests and drinking beer.

Nimble Frost was listening to the suburban males talk about their softball teams, their dogs,

Buffalo Wild Wings, and movie-streaming. Their wives were talking about Instagram and the next community yard sale.

Corporate culture clinging was so chaotically common–

Frost's analog world was fossilized!

Water bottles, smart phones, drones, jobs, and digital coupons... what

they knew and loved and celebrated... was nothing. (But they understood clearly

how to "chill by the pool"... in an organized matrix)

Back to the party–

The rockabilly band–hip young cats with sideburns and tats–

was packing up. The way-cool bass guy asked (politely) Frost to move.

Frost got in his truck, found his way to a Denny's, drank four cups of coffee,

and drove back up the mountain, chilling at Mt Ord, frosty at Christopher Creek,

snug in his rent-by-the-week condo...

Frost, the secular saint, had returned to his monastery...

Still at the diminishing

party, the lovely dreadlock woman thought of Frost but turned her attention to

a soft-bellied thirty-five-year-old market-making bald guy

who was wearing flip-flops, tribal tats, Oakley sunglasses, cargo

shorts, and a Tom Brady jersey. He was loud and proud...

And she felt oddly comfortable with the clone, and was relieved old Frost was

Gone...

Altruistic Hamilton State Community College President Returns Half of Salary

@ Hamilton State Community College

According to a story published on *Outside Postsecondary Ed.com*, a "rogue" community college president has decided he will return half his current salary to the general fund of his institution.

Dr. Luis Glasspar, President of Hamilton State Community College in Santa Klosa, Northern New Mexico, made this stunning revelation at the Northern New Mexico Board of Community Colleges meeting on Wednesday.

According to Glasspar, several factors influenced his decision to return the money, with a genuine call to altruism as the driving force.

"Let me explain," Glasspar told the Board. "My 19,800 square foot house is paid for, my wife Michaela doesn't want her Mercedes convertible anymore, my seven children have completed their university experiences in Switzerland, and I have a hard time spending $766,000 a year (post tax). At retirement in three years, my state pension is secure at $463,462 per annum for life, no matter what I do with my current salary. My family and I talked and agreed that during these troubling financial times, we have a moral imperative to scale back to just what we absolutely need." Glasspar laid out a proposed budget including only his necessities:

$62,000 yearly car allowance and $46,000 travel perks, which would include his wife Michaela's travel when she accompanies Glasspar to conferences. Last year, Michaela provided "executive assistance" for trips including both national and international travel and Hawaii.

Membership in the Northern New Mexico Hot Air Balloon Diners Club–$23,000 dollars monthly.

An allowance for Michaela to cover weekly dog grooming service at the Proper Pooch and Poodle Pretty Pet Pantry.

$750 a week, which is itemized as petty expenditures

Presidential Membership at the Santa Klosa Country Club is traditional, historic, and permanent– and has no connection to other salary package adjustments.

"I have no current control over how my refunded salary monies will be used at HSCC," said Glasspar, although he did express a wish list. "I would hope the college can initiate two strategic action plans—both HR related—both robustly aligned with metrics associated with our mission and values. Perhaps HSCC can provide our 1177 adjunct faculty members a raise. We've been giving them the shaft for several decades. Additionally, our residence hall people need more money. When you get down to it, without the part-timers and RA's, this college, any college, would fall apart in no time."

The NNM Community College Board has organized a 536-member strategic task force, including diverse and gender-neutral consultants and attorneys, to analyze Glasspar's request.

Following a twenty-four-month study of benchmarked presidential salary structures, the Board will announce their recommendations, pending legal counsel and social media input, sometime in early 2022. Glasspar, playing the back nine at Santa Klosa Country Club, was unavailable for further comment.

(Adapted from a Jeffrey Ross story originally printed on the *Cronk News* website)

Professor Frost falls in Love

@The 34 Road near Bear Canyon Lake, Arizona

An increasingly dejected Jack Frost had been napping all afternoon–outside. The weather, once invigorating, was now depressing him. He was cocooned in a sleeping bag on the snowy forest floor, just outside his condo. He had been unable to sleep in the warm building.

So, the reclusive old instructor grabbed a -10 below bag and went outside to get some fresh air–and shiver–and think.

The real reason he couldn't sleep had nothing to do with warm air. Unexpectedly, he was falling in love, way too late in life, and there was nothing he could do. The pain of almost certain rejection was nothing compared to the realization he was helpless–he was about done, just an aged pine in the tired forest...and his ambitions should best be suppressed...or forgotten...

Professor Frost stopped shivering long enough to conceptualize the puzzle. Or at least try to figure out what the puzzle might be. Or if this was a problem rather than a puzzle. What was the deal? So, he was in love–at least by his painful, self-reproaching admission. What did that mean? So trite but so powerful. How did this happen?

He didn't really even know her–in the old non-virtual-reality sense. They were friends on Facebook, and shared similar political and culinary views. Something in her comments made him think he should try to contact her through a different medium. Maybe a phone call or email. He saw potential. His intuition told him *go go go*.

Buzz, his old flame, was a thing of the sordid past. He heard she left Hamilton City and headed east for good..

Love was very confusing. He knew falling in love was just a precursor to a much larger event–coupling. Did he want a romance? Did he want to couple with her? Did he expect her to give up her life and come stay with him on the Arizona rim? Does love ever guarantee a future? And what is a future, anyway? A family photo on the desk at work? Confused, he left that line of thinking.

What should he do? Write a letter? Send flowers to her office?

Email her? Did he have to do something on Valentine's Day? H—, he knew back at Christmas time that he loved her and didn't do anything then. Do the holidays matter? He didn't know her phone number–probably a good thing. Should he make some crazy public comment on Facebook? Bad idea. Really bad.

Maybe, he suddenly realized, he should just let the whole mess go. "Probably the best idea I've had," he murmured into his mitten hands. "But what would the cost be?" The thought of being totally out of her life was devastating. Still, he had to be careful about her foe her own sake. His loneliness was nearly unbearable, but causing her trouble, or discomfort, or pain, or embarrassment–just too much to bear.

He crawled back into his sleeping bag and curled up to get warm. The puzzle was still unsolved.

College Suspends Instruction. President Devotes Full Resources to Rewriting Strategic Plan

@ Southeastern Heber Community College

Dr. Rick Fishinrico, President of Southeastern Heber Community College in Heber, Northern New Mexico, has ordered a stoppage of all instructional activity. SHCC will focus their complete energies on rewriting the institution's strategic goals and core values document.

A fiery and energized Fishinrico made his position clear when he addressed a full cabinet meeting of his VP's, Deans and Directors last week.

"This is the 21st century. Academics are fully supported by technology and ancillary programs. The public wants transparency, accountability, consultants–successful and buzz-rich, corporate stuff. I'm convinced that, with the right vision statement, we can divorce ourselves from the grades 13-14 ashtray image and become a globally recognized higher education leader."

"Our Stakeholders want their money's worth. They want to see synergy between our mission and action plans. I want our staff to be accountable and to show they're worth every penny of those salaries. I've got thirty-two Vice Presidents, each earning 190K a year. I've got fifty-six faculty who average 111K. This brain power needs to work. Organizational learning is far more important than academics. Ask any college president in the country who knows anything. We are who we thought we were."

"Our state-of-the-art online classes are fully automated. We have teachers of record, but our residential faculty spends most days preparing for spring break or baby showers or commenting on Facebook or attending political riots. Yes, these are critical social networking opportunities which facilitate collaborative ventures and friendly hallway conversations."

Clearly college stakeholders demand extensive travel budgets, conference attendance and financial support for all college employees pursuing the doctorate degree in educational leadership."

"Halting all instructional activity will also enable the college to better achieve its performance objectives. Anticipating the Higher Learn-

Ed Commissar's visit (vital for Southeastern's re-accreditation), the college is ever-more committed to continuing the great community college tradition of celebrating best practice theory. To provide evidence of learnedness the college needs time and student-free space to produce infomercials enhanced by videotaped singing deans. Other sustainable activities demonstrated by the 'avatar-friendly' administration remain grounded in futile committee work and senior leadership's historic ability to create, retreat, table and heroically mis-manage crises events and calls for healing."

"By giving the students an unscheduled vacation, we can get more accomplished. What's more important-students or accreditation. And what about brand recognition? I have heard many faculty members say this would be a great place to work without the students–and finding a parking spot will be so much easier!"

"What is more important–organizational learning, mission statements, or students? Ha! I don't know about you, but I like my salary!"

(Adapted from a Jeffrey Ross story originally printed on the *Cronk News* website)

Jack Frost Considers the Movies

@Forest Hills Wandering Minds RV Park

Frost stopped off at an evening gathering in his trailer park. Some suburban types, slumming for the summer in the cool pines (yes, loafing, in a 40-foot gooseneck RV with side outs, microwave, washer-dryer, Bluetooth,) had invited the eccentric over for a cocktail and talk. (Talk to them meant movies and restaurants.)

Frost sat on a fifty-gallon igloo cooler, and he listened to his guests visit about actors, movies they'd seen, the dementia of Hollywood, Spielberg's whereabouts–those kind of things...

Frost wondered about all those actors–and the legacy they would leave.

***

Well, in the deep dark Arizona forest, his hosts and their friends continued through the usual inventory of discussion topics. After listening to this for about an hour, Frost felt a little drowsy. The hostess, noticing he was fading fast, felt the need to be sociable, and queried old Frost–

"Jack, are you ok? You've been very quiet."

Frost warmly, and without regrets, replied, "Oh, I'm fine. I was just wondering. Do you suppose William Wordsworth could have written "The Excursion" if he had lived in these Ponderosa woods instead of England?"

An uncomfortable, almost deathly, silence fell over the group. The host slapped his knee and said, "Ok everybody–c'mon inside. Marge will microwave some popcorn–and we'll get the movie started... Anybody need a drink? Jack, old man, you've had enough!" Big Laughter erupted from the revelers.

Frost went home.

Academic Regalia Event Sparks Controversy

@Copperfield Community College

They're at it again at Copperfield Community. President Dr. Phil Dolly and his institution seem to be a lightning rod for controversy.

Watchdog group *The Academic Regalia Freedom Foundation (ARFF)* has filed a lawsuit hoping to stop a controversial new event planned at one of America's premier workforce development community colleges.

Copperfield Community College recently initiated a new, fully transparent celebration called the Spring Equinox Display of Academic Regalia.

A brief filed by attorneys representing ARFF sourly noted the planned event is "distasteful, disrespectful, profile-based, possibly anti-American and contrary to the innate and traditional purposes of academic regalia."

ARFF members have also privately expressed concern at what Copperfield faculty members might be wearing–or not wearing–beneath their academic regalia. One *ARFF* officer was reported to have said, "Those Copperfield Faculty members give 'free' community college a whole new meaning."

Philip Dolly, president of Copperfield Community College, was shocked that ARFF would take umbrage with his institution's learner-centered celebration.

Dolly posted a fiery reply to *ARFF* on CCC's website: "Our intentions are pure, learned, and noble. Spring is a time of rebirth, of hope and change. By seeing us in our academic garb in the classrooms, in the restrooms, or at the snack bar, students will ask questions about the meaning and history behind the colors and the various degrees. We hope our dog grooming, welding, and truck driving students will be motivated to achieve success, graduate, and soon wear their own regalia at work. Of course, the cap and gown attire may not be appropriate or safe in some learning environs at Copperfield, but we hope for widespread involvement."

Various opinions on the case have mushroomed in the media.

An op-ed piece appearing on the *Outside Post-Secondary Ed* website noted, "*ARFF* is intellectually frozen in the 19th century. *ARFF* seems to think those dour one-use gowns and mortar boards should stay in the closets or hang on hooks behind office doors, covered in drycleaner plastic–except for December and May graduation ceremonies."

A body language expert and psychotherapist on *WOLF News* indicated the Copperfield faculty and administration's apparently bizarre desire to wander aimlessly around the college in academic robes probably was symptomatic of "repressed childhood dress-up syndrome" and noted such behavior as "manifested latent role-playing confusion."

An anonymous source from the Department of Post-Secondary Education said, "The upcoming ARFF court decision might have unpredictable–even dark–consequences for the eventual implementation of the Free Community College policy."

The United States 43rd District Court of Appeals on West Midway Island will hear the case sometime in 2017. Judge Preston Paxton, Chief Justice of the Midway Court, issued a statement saying, "The case revolves around key First Amendment issues that cannot be ignored–even at a community college. I am also concerned that holding the event in conjunction with the Spring Equinox might violate widely-supported separation of church and state policies as well."

Wow. There's always something going on at CCC!

(Adapted from a Jeffrey Ross story originally printed on the *Cronk News* website)

Gert, East Mesa Community College Student and Mother of Seven

@Mesa, Arizona

At 10:30 p.m., Gert poured herself a cup of strong instant coffee and got out her art history book. Her youngest four kids were finally asleep. Gert is thirty-six years old. The kids have three different fathers.

You might say she had been a bit of a party girl back in her late twenties. Gert had been quite happy with her routine—back then she had worked at a Triangle J Food Mini Mart, loved playing darts at the Copper Coin Tavern, could dance on the tables after a few beers, and looked terrific. She was a karaoke queen—and batted .370 on the softball field. Her nickname had been *The Fly*.

Her parents wanted her to go on to college, or cosmetology school, after she finished her GED, but she would hear nothing of it. Gert had boyfriends (lots of 'em), backstage passes to almost every rock concert in Hamilton City, and some great legs.

She even worked as an exotic dancer for a few years, but after a snake bite gave her an infection, she quit. (She had also been startled to see her old funny dad in the crowd one night, boozy and leering, paying one of her big, bouncy-bosomed friends for a lap dance...)

Now, fifteen years later, Gert was holed up in a twenty-six-foot travel trailer with her kids, living on welfare and aid to dependent families, worried about her snake-sized varicose veins and bleeding gums, and desperate to get a job. Her looks were gone, her teeth hurt, and the kids were always hungry.

Recently, one of her community college teachers, Dr. Seemy, told her (shouted at her in a high-pitched voice) to Never Give Up!

Gert enjoys speaking to Dr. Seemy about her troubles. She wants to be like Dr. Seemy someday and have money and brains. Gert has started wearing black sequin framed eye glasses in homage of Dr. Seemy.

Gert is about done, about worn out. She has no idea why she needs calculus and art history and chemistry to be a massage therapist, but someone at the college, some big wheel, some Dr. Elvis Perkins or Patches or Paxon or somebody, changed the requirements, and now she is having big-time trouble finishing her thirty-credit hour (now forty-one credits) certificate.

Gert couldn't study. *I'm just too tired. I don't know if I can take another hour of class with that Dr. Chicken, either. That guy is a total bore.*

This was her second try at art history, her third try at calculus (after taking five pre-requisite math classes over seven years), and her first attempt at chemistry–which she was failing. She was tired of tutoring, tired of being poor, and, well, just plain tired.

Gert had spent nearly eight years working on what should have been a one-year massage therapy program. *How can it be?*

Thank God I've been receiving Pall Grants, been able to get school loans, had federal and institutional work-study jobs, and renewable Men of Diverse Purpose Club scholarships–or these last eight years would have been tough.

Pushing through the door, Gert lit up a filtered Camel and gazed at the stars.

On the slab next to her trailer squatted her 1989 Hoondah four door sedan, with three flat tires, a shattered rear windshield, busted transmission, faded smiley face decal, and frozen motor. Nearly fossilized in rust, it had nurtured her sense of financial inadequacy for years now...

And I can't pay the rent money tomorrow, either.

About six minutes later, her oldest child, carrying a brand-new vampire novel and a can of house-brand soda, hungry and unable to sleep, found Gert, passed out, propped up against the trailer, cigarette still burning in her fingers, snoring and drooling...

(Originally published in *College Leadership Crisis: The Philip Dolly Affair* Rogue Phoenix Press, 2011 by Jeffrey Ross and Jann M. Contento)

Thirteen Ways of Looking at Community Colleges

A poem by Prof Jack Frost

@ Silver State Technical Community College, Room F134

With special Thanks to Wallace Stevens

I
Sprawling fifteen city blocks
The county's only postsecondary thing
Was the campus of the college.
II
The college had three challenges
Each lovely
Academic, Workface, and Developmental education
III
Tired cars overheat in summer parking lots
A small slice of daily dreams
IV
Academic and Workforce
Are one
Academic and Workforce and Community College
Are one
V
What do stakeholders desire,
Prestige of higher education
Or utility of vocations
The students graduating
with certificates–or degrees?
VI
Learners who text and tweet
In unrepentant manner
Their iPhones fresh and gloating
Emboss the tired teacher

Her class
Reshapes assessments
–And outcomes make no promise.
VII
Oh, sleepy men of Instruction
Why do you dream corporate careers?
Can you not see how the college
Depends on yearly taxes
And the will of those that pay you?
VIII
We hear the noble speakers
And focus groups and missions
But we know, too
books–and trades–must somehow matter
While we toil and teach our classes.
IX
When the college expanded mission
The budget stretched and tattered
And the staff took pay cuts to maintain
X
At the sight of Grecian athletes
Competing on the track
The mayor shook his head in wonder
And called the local high school.
XI
The instructor flew towards NISOD
To receive his medallion
Still Fearful of the greater teachers
Who made their online way
In the postsecondary glimmer
Of the Colleges
XII
The budget is moving
The deans must be meeting.
XIII

It was articulation all afternoon
And the committees reached agreement
Most courses would transfer
The universities sat and signed the papers
For they need enrollment, too.

(Adapted from a Jeffrey Ross poem originally printed on the *Cronk News* website)

Barry Woodwurd, Counselor

@ Copperfield Community College

Mr. Woodwurd works steadily and without ceremony. He might have had a career in minor league baseball, but he chose instead to provide academic and career counseling to community college students. After working at an intemperate Alaska college for a few years, he came to CCC without fanfare–and has flourished in a steady work kind of way.

He belongs to a few organizations–and attends a conference or two every year or so–but would always prefer to help students rather than spend time networking or hobnobbing. He has a flip phone, true, but he has not set up the voice mail function since buying it seven years ago.

There is not much to say about Mr. Woodwurd. He does not draw attention to himself, or find self-definition in community college culture, or compete in the parking lot. He would tell you he has an analog, rather than digital, orientation to the universe, and he finds the increasingly self-aggrandizing worlds of Facebook and karaoke mildly painful and misguided.

He reads the *Hamilton County Democrat* each morning before heading to CCC. Sometimes he rides a bicycle to work. Sometimes he drives his car. Sometimes he walks. Barry waves to retired Professor Hose when he sees him sitting on his front porch, quietly resting with Wilbur the Duck. (Mr. Hose never waves back but stares blankly off into space. Sometimes Wilbur quacks and smiles.)

Barry has a full life outside the community college, but he gives his work day complete and uncompromising attention.

He is a favorite among the CCC staff and students. If something needs to happen, he will get it done the right way without questioning or complaining. Never a windbag, never needing attention, he just works effectively, with integrity and vigor. Typically, he advises seventeen to twenty students per day. He has posters of Jackie Robinson and Carl Yastrzemski decorating his office. "Great men," he shrugs. "They were great players too."

Western Columbia University educated (MA, Student Personnel), he is sharp-dressed, charming, some would say handsome, and too often self-deprecating. Mr. Woodwurd can almost always be found in his CCC office working with students. Sometimes he can be found, after work, shooting a few baskets over in the gym.

Married and happy, he does not gossip, seek status, or complain. A true communitarian, he is at peace with himself and his decisions. An intrinsic *steward* rather than a self-professed leader, Mr. Woodwurd does his job well and then goes home to his family and friends. Quietly.

(Originally published in *College Leadership Crisis: The Philip Dolly Affair* (Rogue Phoenix Press, 2011) by Jeffrey Ross and Jann M. Contento)

Dr. Hill's Story

@ Lone Tree Community College, Lone Tree, Nebraska

Prelude

Dr. Hill drove away from the small-yet-lovely-campus feeling weary. The late summer Nebraska air was hot and humid, but not nearly as thick and oppressive as the meeting he just left. He enjoyed his work, his teaching, his students, but the daily grind was another matter. He had been in this business so long that even software upgrade training and social justice issues were starting to simmer like old news. Higher education seemed to be moving farther away from teaching and learning and academics. He wasn't sure what has happening. Things were different now. But he had no dog in that fight. And he was a man of scholastic peace. It was the Friday before Labor Day weekend, and he had three days off before the fall semester began.

He would admit these days he was more interested in reading about new solar panel designs than hearing about online tutoring chat rooms.

Samuel Hill turned up the radio in his old jeep and caught the last few bars of "Cat scratch Fever" on a Grand Island FM Station. The song reminded him that he was going to start an article questioning the significance of rock music in western culture. He wondered when rock music would decline in popularity. Probably when the last boomer passed. Or it became politically incorrect.

He still didn't use his phone to play music. Nor did he own an iPod.

The old jeep radio wouldn't support an aux cord anyway. Any notion of playlists and buying songs appeared odd to him. Reflecting, he realized he might have purchased a few LP's back in the old days. And maybe an eight track or cassette tape. But not many. He wondered when free FM broadcast radio would finally be finished. He knew satellite fee-based radio was very popular these days. And iPhones were filled with downloaded songs. Oh well.

Prof. Hill was going through a period of change and adjustment. Just four short months ago, Samuel Hill had retired from his full-time faculty job at Copperfield Community College back in North New Mexico. That thirty-year career of grading essays had finally concluded. Phew. It had been burdensome. CCC had given him a good life–just not the life he had expected. Sure was a fast thirty years, he thought, as he turned down the gravel road to his new home. He was starting a fresh chapter. He was looking forward to his new circumstances.

Back in May, he had driven his motor home (pulling his jeep along) to see his old friend August Nightingale in Nebraska, and somehow ended up staying–by sheer good luck. He was now starting a part-time teaching position at Lone Tree Community College, close to the Platte River.

When he first arrived in Nebraska, in early June, the now semi-retired Doc Hill had spent about a week in Aurora, just twenty miles to the south of Lone Tree, with his RV parked out in front of Nightingale's home. For a day or two, he and the Nightingales enjoyed catching up on Copperfield and Hamilton city news. Nighty and his wife, Sarah, had each lived in Hamilton City earlier for many years. Nightingale had worked at Copperfield for a time. Nightingale had been a policy researcher for the college, and Sarah had worked in the community for an accounting firm.

Dr. Hill was amazed the couple got along so well. She had helped Nighty convalesce after he was in an auto accident, and they had fallen in love and married a year or so later. They were infatuated with the area and were keen on the "healing" qualities possessed by small Midwestern towns.

An old, confirmed bachelor by default, Hill had never really admired or understood the domestic situation embraced by most. But the Nightingales were generous, pleasant people. And he learned a great deal about the local area from them. At the time, he had no idea he would soon be one of their neighbors–though a short distance away.

Now, in very early September, he "lived" in a small studio cabin on the banks of Pi Lake–a water filled sandpit not far from Lone Tree–and about twenty miles north of Aurora. He rented the red cabin from an attorney in Sioux City. The place had a nice porch, a pot belly stove, a loft, a kitchen, and a bathroom. Dr. Hill's motor home and jeep were kept nearby in a western movie set-like stand of cedar trees, under a large cotton wood, sheltered from the late summer sun. He was only to live in the cabin for one year, but he liked it. He liked it a lot. The place was a getaway for the attorney and his wife, but they were traveling in Europe for a time and were happy to find a tenant.

While visiting the Nightingales in Aurora, Hill had espied an ad in the local paper about adjunct teaching openings at LTCC. At about the same moment, he saw the Pi Lake cabin for rent notice. The coincidence was amazing. He thought it would be Thoreau-like, almost romantic, to live in a cabin on the banks of a lake.

Apparently, the college had a section of American Lit Survey that needed an instructor. And the attorney was anxious to find a tenant for his cabin before he flew to Berlin. A couple of Skype interviews and phone calls later, both deals were consummated. When things came together, Dr. Hill was ecstatic–and almost relieved. He had a cabin on the lake, and a nice teaching job to keep him engaged with the academic world.

Transition

Dr. Hill enjoyed drinking a cold lemonade and listening to the cattle lowing in the evenings at Pi Lake. Dusk-time birds and bats flitted about the salmon-colored sky, finding a meal, acrobats against the greying pinks and blue. This lake residence was perfect. A constant gurgling and murmuring of the inlet stream, the wail of a suspect mountain lion late at night, the slap of beaver tails on the calm water surface–these sounds were more potent, more musical, than any symphony to the newly part-time employed English professor.

While his recently-retired colleagues rode tour busses around Brussels, or hoped for sanctuary in San Francisco, or wandered around Times Square looking at signs, he dipped his old toes into the lake–and felt redeemed. The cattle, the grasshoppers, the gymnastic butterflies–none cared a hoot for politics, careers, or gossip. But the whisper of cedars and poplars on a breezy day–surely the music of the spheres, the stuff of stars.

Pi Lake formed when sand was dredged out from a pit near the Platte River. The Platte, a mile wide and an inch deep, meandered down from the Rockies and into Nebraska, finally committing itself to the Missouri River near the city of Plattsmouth. A geologist would tell you the river's sandy banks and valley were the eroded remnants of those vast mountains to the west. Hill thought, more poetically, that the Platte represented a little slice of western desert cutting through the rich, black, fertile Nebraska farmland. He had even discovered a beat-up looking small prickly pear in a bluestem grass stand one morning while hiking around the lake.

But cacti were rare here in Merrick County. Along the river bottom and tributaries and lakes, cedars, poplars, cottonwoods, and grasses were plentiful. Hill found this be a magical environment.

The cabin sat about twenty yards above the waterline. Some very nice maple trees planted back in the seventies by the attorney's grandfather made for a majestic shade pool. There was a pump house sitting just off to the east of the cabin. A floating boat dock stretched out about ten feet from the shore. Sometimes Dr. Hill would sit in a lawn chair on the dock and use a cane pole and bobber and worms to catch bluegills...and think about the book he intended to write.

Dr. Hill hoped to write a novel, some sort of powerful literary work, during his first year of retirement. Or maybe the second. This was a daunting, a haunting task for him—his plan to begin was always on the back burner while ideas swam around in his head like a school of crappies. Oh, he had notes scattered around on pieces of paper, and character outlines on his laptop, and visions dancing before him almost hourly. But beginning this project was difficult. Not because he couldn't write.

During the last ten years, he had written and published numerous Op-eds on community college purpose and higher education in general, and "scads" of articles on teaching practices and curriculum ideas Ho hum. He had tried to publish his many poems—but to this point had no success. He had neither the gift of jangly marketing verse—or the academic MFA training to churn out those word-melded poems nobody but other grad students could understand. In his more rational moments, he realized the poetry-rejections had a lot to do with his inability to successfully generate his novel. He wanted to be an artist (heart), but he seemed to be a craftsman only (head).

Dr. Hill knew another community college professor who struggled with the art-making complex. His friend Adam Bliss, back in Hamilton City, had left the teaching world to become a musician. It didn't work out.

Crazy Bliss had a good teaching job somewhere in the Midwest, gave it up, and now worked as a maintenance man in a trailer park and tried to promote himself as a patio singer at local restaurants and taverns. Hill had lost touch with Bliss as of late, but he remembered going to see him play at a Moonbucks once or twice. He also remembered Bliss nervously glancing at the tip jar, which was empty. No one was paying attention to him while he croaked out sort of interesting acoustic versions of Def Leppard songs. Dr. Hill always thought Bliss was too old and too nutty to think he could make it as a musician, but whatever. His choice of songs, and the context, seemed to be at odds too. Dr. Hill remembered, suddenly, that Bliss had a bad reputation around Hamilton city as a "ladies' man"–especially with married women. Hmm.

Well, I'm not Bliss, he thought to himself. Those pretend musicians are all crazy anyway. I have a little bit of a publication track record. I just need a creative scaffold to get moving on this thing. Just some kind of hook to hang my hat on.

Hill liked to think about the art and craft dichotomy. Probably too much. One of his favorite authors was Edgar Allen Poe (a writer and a poet). In grad school, Dr. Hill had learned that Poe was not part of the moral tradition (Thoreau, Whittier, Emerson) of the 19th century–rather, he was an aesthete, an artist, who sought to reunify a broken reality in most of his short stories and poems–Poe made great art out of macabre themes. This notion of unifying art and living–enjoying an aesthetic rather than a crafted life–well, it haunted old Hill. Somehow, in his forthcoming novel, he wanted to work out that theme, that motif. Not the life of an artist, or of a person who enjoys looking at paintings in a gallery, but a life combining an aesthetic sensibility with morality. And so far, he just couldn't figure out what to do... But he thought living in a nice idyllic setting, and teaching a section of American Literature at Lone Tree CC might get him inspired. Sure.

Dr. Hill enjoyed sleeping on the patio of the red cabin. The area was fully enclosed and had several large windows that could be opened for fresh air. The view of the lake was perfect from the patio. Hill enjoyed early mornings images the best. He could watch fish jumping and birds dipping at the surface of the water before the day revved up. On some mornings, equally pleasing, the lake at sunrise was mirror smooth and untroubled.

He liked to recline on a cot, covered by a blanket or two, always wearing a pair of shorts. He sensed fall weather would force him back into his motor home, but he thoroughly enjoyed his sleeping arrangements during the summer.

Hill was quite fortunate to have worked so long as an educator–and to have earned a decent state-funded pension.

He put his feet up on an old Pennzoil bucket he found in the pump shed and threw a fish line with a bobber. Ahh! Back to the classroom next week. But this moment was perfect. Speaking out loud to the trees, he said earnestly, "Why do people work all their lives? So they can retire and sit by a lake drinking an ice-cold lemonade? The truth was with them always!" Old retired Dr. Hill was a very happy man. If he could just stay away from meetings!

#PiratesforPay Part-time Faculty Walkout

@Eastern Omaha Community College

Prof Richard Hose was sweating profusely in the mid-September late afternoon Omaha sun. He and 273 other adjunct (part-time) faculty were marching back and forth between the parking lot and administration building at Eastern Omaha Community College. They were on the third day of an organized strike. Each wore a black t-shirt with a skull and crossbones image emblazoned on the front and back. Hose, the ringleader, wore a stylish three-cornered black and silver pirate hat and carried a toy parrot on his shoulder. Most of the dissidents carried signs: "Slavery ended in 1863 "; "Give me Bennies or I'll be Dead"; "We're doing this for the students"; "#PiratesforPay"; "Stop the cultural salary appropriation!"; "Viva Socialism!"

Some motorists leaving the parking lot honked and waved in support of the movement. Most gave the marchers the middle finger and shouted angrily about how the hapless employees were interfering with traffic flow in and out of the college. Four passionate Marxist students had marched with the professors on the first day, but only the tired and sagging part-timers remained on this this third and pivotal day of the event.

The movement was outraged and demanded justice. The adjuncts had simply endured enough. Decades of lousy salaries and administrative puffery had finally called them to action. Adjunct faculty were paid $650 a credit hour for teaching at EOCC–$1950 for a three-credit hour course lasting from mid-August to early December.

At one Adjunct Action Meeting, a frustrated biology professor shouted out, "Fight for $15? Hah! I'd be happy to get $5 an hour! I can barely afford to drive out here to teach–and I sure can't afford to buy a #$%$#@@ Moonbucks cup of coffee. #PiratesforPay! #PiratesforPay! #PiratesforPay!"

They had no health insurance, campus offices, or recognition. Now, they would force the administration to meet their demands–or else. They could only teach nine credit hours a semester, according to strict benefit thresholds for part-time employee guidelines, so an adjunct teaching six classes (eighteen credits) during the school year would earn $11,700. Compare this to the thirty-seven assistant and associate deans and VPs each making over $175,000 a year!

The residential faculty (full-timers), who averaged only $88,000 a year in salary, lauded the effort of the part-timers, but none joined them in the walk out. They were quite comfortable with their own salary packages and didn't want to rock the boat too much since most hoped to be deans in a year or two anyway.

Of course, there had been meetings–with deans, other administrators, and even the governing board. Individuals and gr oups were, of course, sympathetic to the issues of low pay and no bennies. The thirty-member Deans Council listened to Hose respectfully when he addressed their recent meeting. (For effect, he wore his pirate suit and took his parrot along!) His eighty-five-slide PowerPoint was compelling.

In the discussion that followed, they promised to make recommendations to the appropriate VPs, form focus groups, survey students, and further assess the role of Contract Faculty within the spectrum of the Mission Statement and Core Values at EOCC. The knowledgeable professorship and administrators sensed a symbolic one-day work stoppage might help get the public's attention. Even the fat-cat full-timers enjoyed sticking it to "The Man" occasionally!

Soon after, the Governing Board patiently listened to the Pirate's demands for better pay–then the College's legal counsel addressed the group and advised them there was no more money. They had signed contracts, knew the salary range, and simply needed to apply for full-time positions with the district if they wanted more compensation.

Finding no satisfaction in negotiating or due process, the Pirates walked out on their classes Monday the 5th. Now, late Wednesday afternoon, no demands had been met, but the group felt very good about their strategy and perseverance.

Hose was tired, thirsty, and hungry. Even though he had a big belly, his belt had loosened up and his trousers were sagging in the sweaty heat.

He was disappointed no food trucks were on scene–especially since the #PiratesforPay organization secretary had called several owner/operators and advised them of the demonstration. (The Food truck operators knew the adjuncts had no money–and didn't want to waste their valuable time at the Pirate demonstration.) Prof Hose had hoped his friends Steve and Kim might have brought their Chicago-cuisine food truck, but alas, no such luck.

Suddenly, the Chief of Campus Police, Lt. Col. Gerry O'Neal, arrived on his golf cart. He pulled out a bullhorn and addressed the long, sweaty, courageous line.

"Protestors! You are hereby ordered to disperse pursuant to OECC Policy 1006A-Unlawful Assembly! I will give you thirty minutes to get out of here, or our officers will begin making arrests."

Groans of disbelief erupted from the passionate but discouraged academics. They had come so far!

"Come on, Jerry–the admin knows we are doing this. They were supportive of the idea," moaned the disbelieving chief Pirate.

"Dick, I know, and I don't want to arrest you. But here's the thing. Enough students dropped your classes that every course taught by adjuncts was cancelled because of low enrollment. So, you have all been terminated–and now you are trespassing."

Unable to afford much jail time, the #PiratesforPay organization morosely found their way out of the parking lot in their early nineties era automobiles and headed to the unemployment office. A moral victory... Justice was served! Ahrrrrr! Dick Hose took off his pirate hat and focused on the positive. Maybe Quicky Mart had a position opening!

Adjunct Faculty Salary Taxonomy

@Copperfield Community College

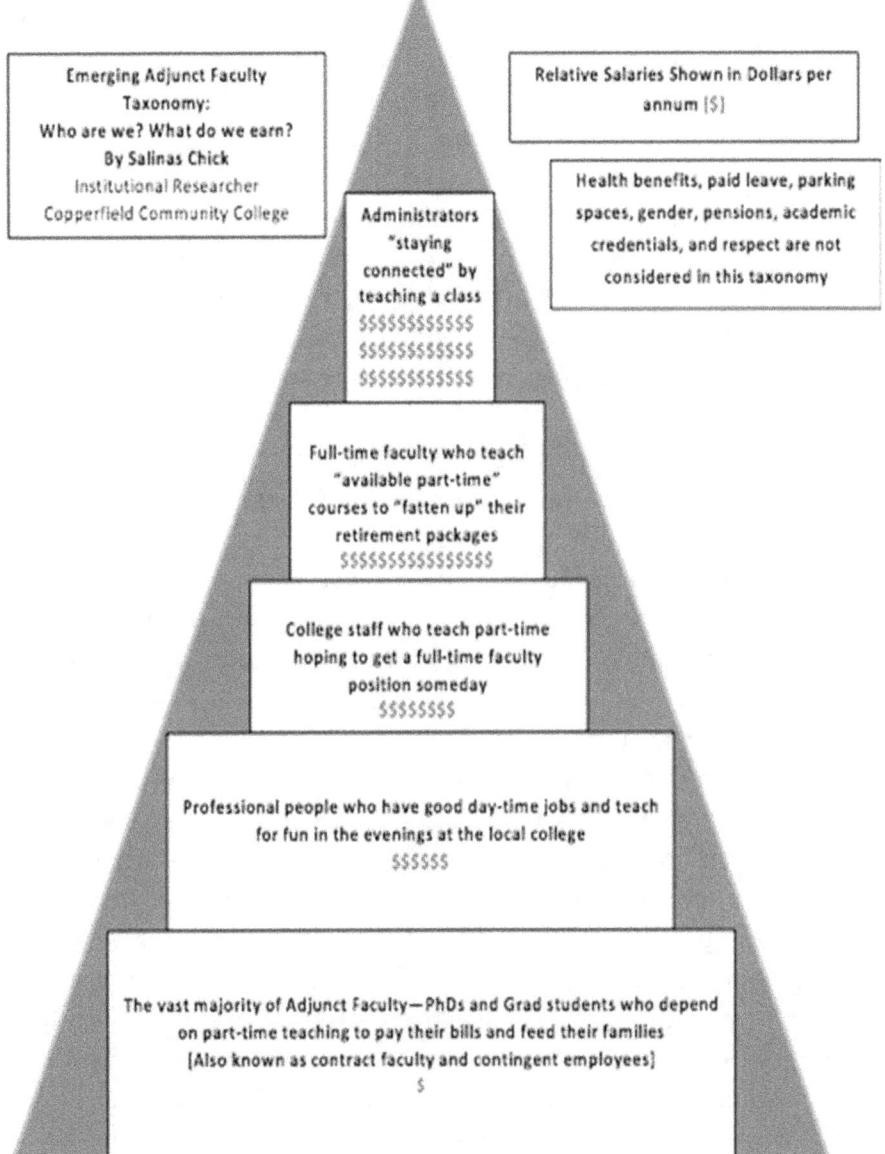

Emerging Adjunct Faculty Taxonomy:
Who are we? What do we earn?
By Salinas Chick
Institutional Researcher
Copperfield Community College

Relative Salaries Shown in Dollars per annum [$]

Health benefits, paid leave, parking spaces, gender, pensions, academic credentials, and respect are not considered in this taxonomy

Administrators "staying connected" by teaching a class
$$$$$$$$$$$
$$$$$$$$$$$
$$$$$$$$$$$

Full-time faculty who teach "available part-time" courses to "fatten up" their retirement packages
$$$$$$$$$$$$$$$$$

College staff who teach part-time hoping to get a full-time faculty position someday
$$$$$$$

Professional people who have good day-time jobs and teach for fun in the evenings at the local college
$$$$$$

The vast majority of Adjunct Faculty—PhDs and Grad students who depend on part-time teaching to pay their bills and feed their families
[Also known as contract faculty and contingent employees]
$

Taxonomy by Jeffrey Ross originally Published by *Cronk News*

Psych Professor Archives Novelist's DNA

@Western South Iowa Community College

Dr. Alexandra was in a conundrum. He was staring at the opened manila mailing envelope resting on the card table in his small living room. About twenty minutes ago, he had opened the envelope and removed the book inside.

Fritz Alexandra, PhD psychology, had undergone a complete emotional turnaround in the last few moments.

Old Fritz had been quite pleased to receive the signed copy of the detective story. Two weeks ago, he had ordered the text directly from the author, who lived over in Indiana, and she had been kind enough to sign the copy. But the confident bachelor professor had been greatly affected by seeing her signature and her printed address on the envelope.

His elation at receiving the book and seeing her handwritten encouraging words on the second page ("Best Wishes"), suddenly vanished. This happened when he picked up the slightly-torn envelope and held it over the small recycle bin in his kitchen.

The learned professor realized, or seemed to determine, that the author's DNA might be somewhere on the envelope. The postage was metered, true, so she did not affix any stamps. But she must have handled the package, and she surely opened the book to sign it.

The good doctor was too fond of her, too close to her through her stories, to throw her DNA out. He had seen her picture. She was beautiful, poised, and sophisticated. The thought of her DNA heading off to a recycling plant in Des Moines or Davenport was just too much for him.

He sat back on a folding chair, aghast at his obsession. Still struggling with his feelings, he looked closely at the book and saw no special or cryptic message. He waved it under his nose but smelled no perfume. (He only inhaled paper and ink aromas.). Frantic, he looked for a lock of hair, or a business card, or a scribbled phone number. Nothing. Significantly, he found no lip stick smudges.

Agitated, he lunged for a tall-boy beer and drank it in fifteen seconds. The professor always kept a few nearby in an ice chest.

He peered inside the envelope, hoping to find any, any at all, message or sign. Nothing. He drank another beer and then fished around in a desk drawer for a pack of Pall Malls. Lighting two, he inhaled deeply, and felt better. His empiricist-self compromised. Tomorrow, he would buy an 8 x 11 picture frame with a glass cover and preserve her iconic DNA forever.

He felt better after thinking about the envelope preserved within the picture frame, and the professor was able to go to bed. But he set the envelope on his night stand and stared happily at her address while finishing his smokes.

Finally, convinced her DNA was to be safely archived, Alexandra was able to fall asleep. Good thing too. Tomorrow, he was going to have a big day. Dr. Alexandra was beginning a new noon luncheon lecture series called "How to Tell if Your Relationship is Healthy," and he really needed some rest.

Laptop Josh, Student

@Copperfield Community College

Laptop Josh could be seen at the campus Moonbucks, or on a patio, or on a bench, nearly every day at CCC. He always had his laptop and a Bible with him–and a cup of Moonbucks Supremo Iced Coffee. No one knew for sure if Laptop Josh was enrolled in any courses at CCC.

Rumor had it that he was a preacher–or a musician–or Russian agent–or maybe a socialist of some kind. His Hoondah car had several dents and was without hubcaps. The tires looked very iffy but he kept the interior clean.

Before he was banned form the CCC campus for expressing his First Amendment rights, the bartender, Henry Mc Dougal, could frequently be seen discussing politics with Laptop Josh, usually on a bench outside the administration building. The pair would be shouting, waving their arms, and sometimes arguing about Christian Democrats, A.O.C., global cooling, socialism, and Intelligent Design.

Dean Preston and Campus Director Clarissa Vasquez, when walking and talking together, always greeted the personable Laptop Josh. And he always cheerfully and graciously acknowledged their hello.

("Such a nice student," cooed Clarissa into Preston's left ear, the one without the diamond earring, one late afternoon.)

Laptop Josh, a man of great patience, has five daughters–all young women now–all beautiful and intelligent. Seven or eight presidents at CCC had made inquiries about Laptop Josh's identity and purpose. Laptop Josh has outlasted them all...

(Based on a story originally published in *College Leadership Crisis: The Philip Dolly Affair,* Rogue Phoenix Press, 2011 by Jeffrey Ross and Jann M. Contento)

Father John, World Religions Adjunct at Copperfield Community!

Father John, adjunct faculty member, wearily slumped over the rough and cracked steering wheel of his rusty old Ford Bronco after his Tuesday night World Religions class. He smashed another Lucky Strike into the debris-laden ash tray and sighed deeply.

In many ways, the night had been typical–the heating and cooling systems had worked in opposition all evening–making the room, at times, unbearably hot–and then nearly

Arctic-like when the a/c unit kicked in. [He had mentioned this to the custodial staff and learned the controls to the unit were located seventy-two miles away at a technology device controls center at IBC over in Roswell]. "Sorry Father–we've been looking into this for fifteen years!"

The internet was down. A howling wind outside blew leaves into the classroom whenever someone opened the door. Fluorescent bulbs flickered with minds of their own.

Students had straggled into the class late and had been disinterested in his lecture on the Dao. But tonight, something had somehow been different. One of "God's Marines," Father John, a Jesuit, was up against a difficult foe. He was beginning to realize the enormity of his task at this community college. A few weeks into the semester, he had begun to fully, completely, see his situation.

Ach, laddie, the picture wasn't pretty.

Tonight, the college servers were down, his email was inaccessible, and only one light worked in his classroom. Plus, he could hear pounding music coming through the wall from the Music Appreciation class next door.

And then, well, his students always presented him with challenges.

There was Rudy, a big strapping red-headed boy with tattoos and a Billy Goat beard who worked as a welder in the day time and dozed off during class. He'd been in the navy. He had a great future ahead of him if he could survive the present!

Oh–and Mary, a young mom with numerous piercings and lavender hair who texted secretively [with a furrowed brow and pursed lips] off to nowhere. She believed in learning by physical osmosis: that by simply occupying space, her learning and career needs would be met.

And Angel? He was formerly a fine specimen of a lad who had nearly been destroyed by liquor and smokes and dance clubs. He often came to class smelling of drink and cheap perfume, and he never made it through the evening session without sneaking out the door to smoke.

Father John was from Nabob County–part of the Albuquerque Diocese. He had convinced the Bishop of his plan to teach one class at CCC and to have the adjunct salary donated back to his home church, San Rafael, for the food bank. The trip to Hamilton City was nearly 170 miles one way–and difficult in stormy weather, but Father John was able to stay overnight at the rectory of St. Thomas Aquinas Church nearby. He knew that Copperfield had a reputation for academic excellence–he remembered reading Dr. Phil Dolly's opinion piece in the *Duke City News* about CCC's future as a higher education leader.

He had seven students remaining in his course [from the 22 originally enrolled], but he was optimistic. Their diversity was intriguing.

Another of his students was Ricky–evidently a very bright student in high school who was clearly not ready for an academic course such as World Religions. Father John did not provide for Extra Credit assignments usually, but for this class….

Cynthia, a friendly and cheerful young lady, talked all class, and her vocabulary was quite good, but she had turned in no work to date.

Trevor was a high school senior, a dual enrollment student, who drew *Call of Duty* stick figure cartoon pictures [with a flair] and constantly shared them with Father John.

Smiling, Father John thought of Kimbon–a very pleasant, charming, and intellectually-gifted woman from Nigeria who simply could not speak or write English. Father John had sent several emails to the Helping English Language Learners [H.E.L.L.] program director about Kimbon's situation, but he had as of yet received no replies.

Father John had recommended, to his students, computer programs, the tutoring center, online tutoring, and private conferences–all to no avail.

Well, he thought, I think I'll stop off at the Copper Coin Tavern on the way over to the rectory and consider this situation further! At least I'm raising some money for the food bank!

Father John ended up having a great time at the Copper Coin. He argued politics for a while with the Scottish socialist bartender, Mc Dougal [a good Catholic but a bit off the beaten path, thought the Father]. He sat down next to Coach Ski at the bar–the CCC football defensive coach was sipping a Canadian Club with just a splash of water and enjoying a pitcher or two of good cold draft beer after a late practice.

Coach Ski asked if the Father could bless the team. "No, lad, I'm a Jesuit. You'll need a Franciscan for that!" They laughed together. When Ski learned Father John was a Fighting Irish football fan, he bought the cleric an Irish whiskey or two. Before long, they were arm and arm singing the Notre Dame Fight Song.

(Three hours, three whiskeys, and six pints later, Father John called Uber.)

Father Francis, parish priest at St. Thomas Aquinas Church, had received word from the Copper Coin Barkeep that Father John would be arriving around one thirty a.m.

When the driver delivered the weary priest, Father Francis led Father John to a cot and tucked him in. He seemed to understand the situation. "Well, John, laddie, 'tis not the seminary ya be teaching at."

Father John, tired, a bit tipsy, but apparently repentant, whispered something.

Perhaps he is praying, thought Father Francis. Sure, he wants forgiveness for such a night! Father Francis bent over to listen, but the words escaped him.

Father John raised himself up on one arm and whispered something again, still not quite audible to mortal man.

The moment was eerie. Suddenly, crickets stopped chirping, mists rolled into the room through the open window, and the numerous luminous, glowing votive candles stopped flickering. Time itself seemed to stand still as the priest tried to speak ....

"Please, Father, speak more loudly," the parish priest further encouraged Father John– and then he leaned even closer to hear, nearly falling over onto the cot himself.

With a smile on his face, Father John [his old hairy, hoary face barely visible in the dim room, his red and rheumy eyes gleaming with fire] began chanting in a sing song voice–

"Wake up the echoes cheering her name…"

"Wake up the echoes cheering her name…

"What's that now Johnny? Wake you up when–oh, lad, God Bless, ya, John, you are at Copperfield now, not Notre Dame," said a laughing Father Francis.

"Get a good night's rest boy and come to confession tomorrow."

[Sidebar– The cost of the Uber ride home, and the subsequent next-day towing expense of Father John's rusty Bronco, negated his semester's salary contributions to the Albuquerque diocese.]

(Based on a story originally published in *College Leadership Crisis: The Philip Dolly Affair* (Rogue Phoenix Press, Salem OR, 2011) by Jeffrey Ross and Jann M. Contento)

Angry Professor with a Ball Bat!

@East Coconino National Forest

Prof. Frost watched her drive up,
The old Bronco bounced on the ruts and broken pieces of shale.
Though it was cold outside, she was sleeveless.
Buzz Clocker was smoking a Pall Mall and grunting like a sow bear when she swung open the door and stumbled through the skiffs of snow, carrying a ball bat and cursing...
"I know you're here, Frost!"
"You can't ignore me you–you–there's no d--- safe space for you, you !@#$%". The howling wind blew her words away.
Frost was standing behind a Ponderosa pine tree, a thick one, sipping on a naturally-chilled energy drink and watching her
She careened around the yard, tripping over a stump, swinging the bat at his motorcycle but missing,
Cursing the trailer, the broken bench press–screaming louder than the wind at times... Angry at the weather, her recent eviction, her old boyfriend, herself.
Then, without damage, she crawled back into the Bronco, and bounced back down the hill.
Prof. Buzz was gone...
Frost sat back in his lawn chair, sheltered his beer, and watched the snow fall.
He had papers to grade before tomorrow's class.

JB O'Connor, College Man, at the Book Store

@Copperfield Community College, Hamilton City, North New Mexico

JB had just left the Student Success Center (housed in the Teaching Learn-ed Center) at Copperfield Main.

He had taken a battery of academic placement, career guidance, gender identification, and student government interest inventories.

Young Master O'Connor had spent about twenty minutes with a lady counselor (d---, she's hot!) making course selections and was now walking over to the Business Center Complex to pay his registration fees.

JB had come to this venerable institution of higher learning for various reasons. (But mostly because his dad told him to go back to school or else...) About two days ago, he quit his job at the Sticky Mart and thought he might like to lounge around the house for a while. That same afternoon, while he was home watching the TV and drinking an ice-cold beverage, his dad, John, strode into the house and told him he had to get another job, or join the military, or go to college, or "Get out of the !%$^@! house."

Basically, lazy and not suited for menial labor, JB had been out of high school for four years now and had never really thought about going on to school.

But none of the armed services wanted him because of his inability to read, so college seemed like a good possibility.

Soon after, during a family council, once the shouting and screaming ebbed, his dad encouraged young JB to attend CCC and find himself. "JB, you can get the easy courses out of the way, and we can save some money in case you want to go to a real college someday. I know that CCC is far cheaper than a regular college; I think they charge $350 a semester compared to HSU's $11,600. Look, if you'll enroll in four classes, I'll pay the costs and you can stay at home. Then someday when you decide to go to college, we might be able to afford it."

Despite JB's documented reading problems (and his poor showing on the math placement test), the lady counselor (d---, she's hot!) had urged him to enroll in Art History, History of World Civilizations, Calculus, and Anatomy and Physiology. (She knew these classes needed enrollment or they might be cancelled–leading to faculty complaints about her advising practices and ability). "You can do it, JB," she said, shaking her pretty fist in the air above her head. We'll MAP out an ASS (Academic Support System) for you and make sure you get free tutoring as often as possible from our peer, para, online, embedded, and virtual tutors. You will love it here at CCC. Chiclet?"

His dad had given him the $350 he needed for tuition. With receipt in hand, only three hours later, JB was enrolled. He went to the bookstore to pick up the four textbooks he needed for his classes. JB was a college man just like that. (He thought about buying a CCC t-shirt but knew they weren't considered cool in Hamilton City.)

After walking past stand after stand of cinnamon tea blends, vampire novels, coffee cups, key chains, rulers, stuffed horses, sunglasses, movie DVDs, flash drives, candy bars, paper-thin one-use graduation gowns, CCC logo shirts, get-well cards, and Go-Go Green Posters, he found the ten-feet by ten-foot section reserved for academic text books at Copperfield Community College.

After scrutinizing titles and course section codes, he picked up the books, checked the prices, and called his dad.

"Hey Dad, I'm down here at the book store. Yep, things are going great. The counselor is HOT. Yep, you were right–the tuition was $350. But I'm gonna need some more money. I had to buy four textbooks–they've got CD ROMs and stuff–and the total bill is $846.71 (that includes tax!) for the books. Dad? Dad? Are you still there?"

(Originally published in *College Leadership Crisis: The Philip Dolly Affair* (Rogue Phoenix Press, 2011) by Jeffrey Ross and Jann M. Contento)

Professor Frost is Rich

@Woods Canyon Lake AZ Campground Hwy 260

Old Adjunct Frost is a funny guy.

Or odd. He never puts anything in the recycle bin.

One of his neighbors was critical.

"What the h---, said old Frost.

I'm not a consumer.

I have a flip phone, an AM radio, a four-cubic-foot refrigerator, and a few pairs of jeans and t shirts I bought at a garage sale.

I watch you Chinchillas tearing down the road in them big SUV's, burnin' up the gas for nothing. Where are you going?

What do you know? Shop? Hah. I need a few apples, some milk, peanut butter, corn flakes, bread, vegetables, and dog food. I can get it all in Forest Lakes.

Restaurants? Hah. The out-of-shape people come and go, come and go, eat and spend–and two days later, cannot remember where they have been.

Music? Hah.

How many !@#$% times do you need to hear Lady Ga?

Get yourself a guitar or sax or something. How many trees does it take to make one iPod?

I've got a Bible, Wordsworth, Blake, Stanley Fish, and AR Ammons.

I just finished reading *1040 Taxes Could be Replaced by One-cent Fees* by Ross. A great book that the establishment and tax-preparer industry fears. Hah.

Yep, I live out here along the road in my Quonset hut I and watch you people.

Quite entertaining. Where are you going? What do you Know?

Excuse me while I get back to my bowl of cereal and "The Prelude." Good luck to you. Really. You need it. Bad."

A Professor's Tale

@Copperfield Community College, Hamilton City, North New Mexico

Professor Allworthy was feeling creative this afternoon. After grading a stack of PHI 101 essays, he thought he might return to the draft of his nearly-completed novella. (His students, he had just learned, though nice enough people, just couldn't differentiate between Descartes and Plato.)

Mr. Allworthy, MA Philosophy, Hopeful College, was quite happy to have a job teaching anywhere. He had been a part-time instructor here at CCC for nineteen years now.

During that time, he had successfully aborted three PhD in Philosophy programs (too much reading and writing). Even so, he had cheerfully maintained his fork lift driving career at the all-night discount furniture warehouse in Hamilton City.

Mr. Allworthy had conducted a nicely-stylized academic ritual this past winter when he ignited, in the family barbecue grill, the emerging-yet-marked-up draft of his dissertation on Descartes. He felt quite at ease during this cathartic moment and even felt great joy as his kids came out and cooked chocolate graham cracker Smores over the curling flames of his life's ambition. (*Well,* he thought, *that may be the end of my academic career, but I've still got my book. I just know it will change our lives*). He recited Frost's "*The Bonfire*" as his tome finally incinerated, and the kids went back inside.

Mr. Allworthy was supported by his wife's plastic pot and pan business. Typically, Alice made in-home presentations three nights a week. Her thrift-store clothes were clean, and she was a good worker. She had sold bowls and lids to nearly everyone who worked at CCC and felt oddly connected to the wives of Dr. Dolly and Dean Paxton. (The wives found Mr. Allworthy's wife to be a bit chatty and odd–they couldn't understand why Alice's husband didn't want a full-time job. But some rooted sense of noblesse oblige kept them buying spatulas and mixing bowls from her– especially near the holidays.)

Back to the professor. He was on to something with this novel–and it was big. (Not the biggest, but big!) In his readings of Descartes, Mr. Allworthy had become fascinated with philosophical dualism. (Sidebar: by dualism, we mean the following. Dual [two kinds] of reality exist: 1) An individual's conscious perception of reality and 2) Reality as it exists apart from an individual. Others might call this subjectivity and objectivity.)

Well, Allworthy had this notion that his book would be a best seller in academic circles because he had come to grips with an amazing fact. At the community college, there is no philosophical dualism. All consciousness blends into the pursuit of a singular approach to intrinsic meaning. It seems that his colleagues find value, worth, and a level of contentment in simply being community college employees, participating in an artificial intelligence created by some ancient and vast consciousness. The single mindedness confounded his Kant-like sensibility. The college had only one modality, one purpose, one vision. What was it?

In the true, or intended, platonic subordination of the community college, diversity and stewardship would flourish. Idealism, truth, and beauty would be balanced by Aristotelian commandments: "Thou shall devote the utmost powers to a common social welfare... above pleasure, money... shall ponder and revere the universal laws that bind...use just so much of tools that service requires...thou shall endure hardship...remain steadfast until habit becomes second nature...you shall find a few friends and hold to the social welfare that is the task of man..."

Allworthy's book, his satire, his novella, was an attempt to make meaning out of his chaos. He looked at the clock and saw it was time to head down to the warehouse. But he was filled with warmth—in the novel form, his ideas could be articulated—and perhaps cut a broad swath of righteousness. Because he recognized the lack of duality at the community college, he knew his own core being was healthy and vibrant.

Alice called out, "Don't forget your lunch pail, dear." His son hugged him, and he went out front to catch the 9.40 PM bus.

(Originally published in *College Leadership Crisis: The Philip Dolly Affair* (Rogue Phoenix Press, 2011) by Jeffrey Ross and Jann M. Contento)

Stevie Burch, Business Major

@ Northeastern Sioux City Community College

Stevie was in his second semester of college at NSCCC. He was a very happy nineteen-year-old. He had a good high school experience the previous four years in Sioux City. He had been an excellent student and athlete. Stevie was an Eagle Scout. Currently, he was taking ENG 102, Psych 102, and ECN 202 at the college. He enjoyed the campus and his fellow students very much. The modern campus had many amenities, and Stevie enjoyed his time spent in the classrooms and social spaces.

Stevie lived at home with his parents and older brother. He drove a hand-me-down Suburbia X automobile, and he had a part-time job as a car detailer and the local Hoondah dealership.

After another year at NSCCC, Stevie will transfer down to the Hamilton State University and major in business.

Stevie, because of his decision to attend the local community college, will not incur massive student debt. He respects his professors and believes strongly he is receiving an excellent education. Like many community college students, he was taking advantage of the low cost and excellent education afforded to him by the local institution. He was asked to try out for the NSCCC baseball team but declined, indicating to Coach Skeeter that he wanted to focus on academics.

His dad, David S. Burch, a very successful concrete paving machine salesman, is very happy with the college because they are saving so much money. Very happy indeed.

Dr. Jones' Office

@ Copperfield Community College

Dr. Jones, Copperfield Community President (for two more "paid leave" weeks, anyway) was packing her belongings. She was under the watchful eye of a CCC Police Officer. His job was to be sure she didn't pilfer any college property as she visited her office for the last time.

The Governing Board had abruptly terminated Dr. Jones' contract at last night's meeting using the institution's somewhat-vague College Work Environment Employee Compatibility Policy #0666 as cause.

The Board President, Mrs. Hallelujah King, had read a simple two-sentence statement. "The CCC Governing Board has determined Dr. Millicent Jones, CCC President, shall be terminated, effective immediately, according to CCC Policy #0666 College Work Environment Employee Compatibility. Her personal views stand in conflict with the college's published mission and strategic goals."

In the brief discussion that followed, the former President learned she would be suspended from her duties, with pay, for two weeks, and then...

Soon, three Campus Police Officers escorted a strangely untroubled Dr. Jones to her car. She was told she could come back and pick up her belongings the next day.

***

What had happened? The long and short of this story is simple. The otherwise-likeable President had ideas and views that irritated the fantasy-bent faculty. A champion of old-time 1960's values, Dr. Jones believed each community college should serve the local community's needs first. She wanted a return to a strategic plan emphasizing job training and basic literacies. Certainly, she appreciated the arts and "good literature," but Dr. Jones was once overheard saying, "Interpreting Hamlet will never help anybody pay their bills!"

Dr. Jones also got into trouble when she questioned the value of a faculty exchange program with elite South-Central Quebec University. "Yes, French culture and cuisine are interesting, but should we put energy into such projects and partnerships when there are 25,000 people in this county who can only read at the fifth-grade level? Where should our priorities rest? Besides the fact we are not a four-year liberal arts school or even a traditional junior college. We should promote courses and programs that help our students, our local folks, move forward in life so as not to become angry political bloggers or develop a sense of victimization so common to students, and especially faculty, in higher education."

Well, the academic faculty, many of whom had unrealistic desires to teach at a university, could not stomach this blasphemous "attack" on the "higher education leader" culture they perpetuated at CCC. They felt threatened by the President's obvious proclivity for Occupational and Developmental Education. And the chaperones didn't want to give up free trips to Canada each summer! So, they complained, threatened, complained, and finally got their way. The Board didn't care for some of Dr. Jones' expensive work-training budget requests—and so...

***

Officer Lowdin was late for his coffee break. He was a little edgy and uncomfortable. "Dr. Jones, are you nearly finished in here? Looks like you have about cleaned out your desk and files. I don't really want to go through your crates and bags. I've always enjoyed working with you. I'm sure those family photos on the wall are probably your property, but maybe you should leave those college awards and plaques behind. I'll have the purchasing agent come over and do a little scan inventory. I can drop off the rest of your stuff at your house after work."

She nodded in agreement, thanked him, and stacked her crates on a pull cart that emanated Thrift Shop style. A smiling Dr. Jones quickly stepped out the office door, nearly knocked down a custodian who was methodically removing her name plate, and gently rolled her belongings to her Tesla S 100D in the parking lot. Things weren't all together bleak. Not at all.

Dr. Jones had a job in Columbus Ohio at Besser Technical

Community College, as Executive Vice-President, starting in two weeks. Networking, you know.

BTCC had been hoping to hire her for years. And their salary schedule was much better, anyway.

***

Officer Lowdin ambled along toward the Purchasing Office. "Huh," he murmured reflectively, "That's the fifth president we've had in seven years. Man, you got to say the right things to be president around here. Don't know if I'd want that job. Couldn't pay me enough. But they make a lot of money. Well, let me see if I can find Paul Harkins and get him to inventory her office. Crazy. She's a good lady. I think she'll land on her feet. I wonder if that Dean Paxson will end up being the interim Prez?"

Noticing his stomach was growling, Officer Lowdin stopped off briefly at the Student Affairs Building in search of a potluck.

Dr. Hill's Student

@ Lone Tree Community College, Central City

The first day of class went well. LTCC followed a four-day work week. Hill's Lit 210 class was scheduled on T-Th from 9-10.30 am. About nineteen students were enrolled in the course. LTCC, in a rather traditionalist manner, started the regular fall semester the day after Labor Day, so his young scholars were subdued that first Tuesday morning following summer vacation. He was surprised the class mirrored a community college group in terms of demographics–all ages seemed represented.

He made the usual first day speech–talking about the text book, attendance, learning outcomes, and the syllabus. He fired up the LED projector and showed the class how he would use the LTCC RedBoard course management software in the class. He admonished them to use email to contact him and noted that because he was an adjunct, he had no regular office but would be available in the LTCC Adjunct Faculty office for an hour after class if anybody wanted to visit with him. The professor advised them to leave their smartphones alone during class but also realized such advice was futile. He had the students introduce themselves and mention a little about their long-term plans. He paid attention to their brief autobiographical "speeches," but there was a lot of information to process quickly. Hill knew it would take few class meetings to get to know them, but he was usually good with names by the third week or so. He passed out a handout providing information about general themes in 19th century American literature and dismissed the class, feeling really tired after only one hour of instruction that first morning. But he was always glad to get that first day meeting out of the way.

After class, Prof. Hill found his way over to the LTCC Student Union and the café. The Lone Tree Café had a special on–their Famous Lonely Burger, medium drink, and Corny Fries for 4.99. Hill planned to bring his lunch most days, but he decided to splurge on a burger today. First day of school, he mused, and I deserve a treat. Hill was basically a very frugal man.

Dr. Hill really didn't know anyone in the union. Or at the college, for that matter, except for a few of his fellow adjuncts and the division chair. He ate quietly and read through a copy of the handout he had passed out the class earlier–and found a d--- typo. As he was on the third bite of his Lonely Burger (a very tasty half pound of beef smothered in Hundred-Island dressing on onion buns), he noticed someone approaching and standing next to him. He wiped off his mouth and looked up, smiling.

"Hello, Professor Hill," she said directly. "My name is Tammy. I'm in your morning lit class. Is it okay if I sit down with you for a second? I have a question about the handout you gave us."

"Oh, sure, please sit down," mumbled Hill, moving his back pack, fries, drink cup, and iPad. He glanced at her quickly, noticing she was a trim thirty-five-year-old or so blonde lady with a laptop case. "How can I help you?"

She adjusted herself in the stackable dining room chair and gazed at him in a strange manner. After an awkward ten seconds or so, she spoke again. "Dr. Hill, do you remember me? Not from this morning–I mean from Hamilton City and Copperfield Community College. Like maybe ten years ago?"

Hill didn't know what to say. *What a bizarre moment* flashed through his mind. She looked vaguely familiar, but ten years was twenty semesters and 30,000 essays ago. He measured his words.

"Good to see you again, Tammy. Did I have you as a student in a comp class? You do look familiar to me."

"I thought you might remember me. No, I never had you for a teacher. Jack Frost was my English teacher. But I attended the Creative Writing Club meetings a few times. You were the sponsor back then. I really liked your poetry."

Now old Hill thought back to the CWC meetings at CCC, and he did remember her. Yes. Tammy Browning. And he appreciated her remarks about his poetry.

"Sure, now I remember. Wow. Ten years. What brings you to LTCC? Hard to believe we would meet again out here in Nebraska! "

She looked at him reservedly. "My husband, er former husband, Robert, got transferred back here in 2010 or so. I don't think you ever met him. He works for a center pivot irrigation company. Hamilton City is their furthest west office. We actually lived in Aurora, out by the airport, for a couple of years. He got involved with a Marquette farmer's wife and left me. It was kind of messy. But the new romance didn't work out for him, either. Sorry. Too much information for you regardless, probably. Anyway, we got divorced, sold everything, and I moved up to Lone Tree. I have a part-time job here at the school and take a few classes. I'm pretty much over all that now. I just want to move forward."

He listened intently, his heart skipping. Hill had to be careful. "I am sorry to hear about your marriage, but it sounds like you are back on your feet. I am glad you enrolled in the class. No doubt we share some common acquaintances back in HC. Do you know if there is a Creative Writing club here? I am just teaching the one class and need to learn more about the school.

Tammy smiled and stuttered a little. "Y-y-yes, the club is called Voices of Lone Tree. They have their first meeting next week. I think it is posted on the LT home page. I hope you can go..."

Then suddenly, "Well, good to see you Dr. Hill. I have to go to my next class. I am very glad you are my lit professor again. I-I-I hope you will share some of your poems with the class," said Tammy Browning sincerely, smiling, backing away carefully, somewhat befuddled.

"Thanks, Tammy. You have a great day. See you in class." Hill watched her walk away. Then, some of his neurons misfired, short-circuited, cross-fired. Scales fell from his eyes and heart. He suddenly had an idea for his novel—and for living an appropriate life. His tenure at Lone Tree might be just what he needed.

Five Good Reasons to Complete that AA Degree

@Middle Central Arizona Community College

Dr. Bruce Martinez, Dean of Instruction at MCACC, was quite pleased. He had just finished reading a very positive article by one of the faculty at his institution. Dr. Jeffrey Roz was usually a bit of a trouble maker, but this piece, published on *Outside Post-Secondary Ed*, was very inspiring. "Ah, um," said Dr. Martinez. "I will see if I can get him a new MCACC coffee cup from the book store."

Five Good Reasons to Complete That Associate Degree
By Dr. Jeffrey Roz

Program Articulation. Most community colleges, including MCACC, have articulation agreements with local universities that allow associate degree completers to transfer articulated courses and programs.

Terminal Work Force Program Completion. The career benefits of an associate degree for people in nursing, computer, and hundreds of fields should not be overlooked, even for individuals who hold baccalaureate or graduate degrees in other academic fields.

A Rung on the Ladder to Personal Success. An associate degree can be a great milepost of academic success. By completing one a student can take pride in accomplishment and envision a future filled with other academic successes.

Future Career Plans. This is probably not mentioned often, but for students who may someday consider working at a community college, the attainment of an associate degree might help land a job at such an institution.

Immediate Career Advancement. An associate degree is a college degree and is often highly regarded by employers; impacts on lifelong earnings have also been well-documented.

(Originally published by Jeffrey Ross in the *League of Innovation Learning Abstracts*)

After Stories

@ Diners Grove

Grove City

By Jann M. Contento, PhD

Gus

Sitting in his usual corner booth, nearest the cash register and revolving glass entry door, Gus appeared uncomfortable in his mock apron and checked trousers. As toast and coffee eaters lingered, Gus snuffed out his third Kool menthol cigarette into a shallow ashtray while Dvořák's Slavonic dance No. 2. played in his head. He and his brother Nicolaus Gerinopolis had opened the Golden Spoon Diner just over four years ago. They had immigrated to America about a decade earlier, most likely for economic and political reasons. However, this food and beverage business, although necessary, was rather foreign to Gus.

He had studied music at the National and Kapodistrian University of Athens, focusing on violin and piano. Gus had been musically inspired as a young lad when a fifth-grade art teacher had asked the class to draw the music she played for the class (Haydn's Symphony No. 96, *The Miracle Symphony*) through a small record player. First gently and then again with vigor, he was emotionally transformed, impassioned to explore music on a personal level. He studied with V. Ross at the youth conservatory for over six years and qualified for the university. It was at the university that Gus met his wife Callie who studied dance and theatre. Known to play and dance a *Romanian Rhapsody* or two, Gus and Callie were young, handsome, and in love. Both were patrons of theatrical performance. Fittingly, Gus proposed, after two or three ouzos, during the second act of the ballet *Spartacus*.

Now, Callie continues to teach youth ballet and acts in community theatre; Gus's music performance is limited to kids' birthdays or Sunday recitals for his immediate and large extended Greek family. Gus was quite aware that only a select few made the Athens State Orchestra. He dreamt of employing his talents playing symphonic classics as part of a working ensemble. However, many of those opportunities had dwindled after the war. Gus had witnessed several accomplished violinists on street corners playing tourist requests for "pop goes the weasel" and hoping for empty hat tips. After moving to the states, and years of working small nightclubs, weddings, and summer festivals, he and his brother Nicolaus painfully agreed to accept family financial backing and opened the kitchen here in 1962, four years ago.

"Hey Gussie, heard Halsted hit another triple yesterday."

Raising his eyes from the arts and leisure section, Gus shadowed the newspaper away from his face. Nick, clad in a common white grease-spattered linen chef jacket and grey checked hound's-tooth trousers, took a short break from the grill and slid into the brown vinyl booth joining his brother.

"Gussie, that young dishwasher...he's a little sloppy, left water suds on juice glasses."

The two remained silent for quite some time as Gus struck a match to light another smoke. An exposed photo in the "Village Section" of the unfolded paper showed a woman in a flowered hat, accompanying four men in trench coats, hats, and shovel spade, breaking ground on new "junior" college.

"Did ya read about this, Gussie? Suppose to open next August. Some kind of college here."

Gus gazed outside at the damp parking lot through the glass opening near the *Yes, We're Open* sign.

"Must be some democratic idea for neophyte college students... Is it a 'real' college, or just some post high school grade 13-14 school?"

"Not sure, Gussie, says here it's preparation for going to the university. I thought you either go to university, go to the service, or go to work. I guess a kid will find out if he's smart enough for university. This 'junior college' will have all kinds of classes, job training, as well as preparation classes for university. So, kids can transfer these to the university, if they can get in...in a few years. Think it will help business, Gussie?"

Gus graveled his voice a bit and tapped the tip of his Kool menthol on the ashtray.

"Too many choices are not always good for kids or customers for that matter. We've attempted to offer more items to our breakfast, lunch, and dinner menus, but the basics seem to outsell others. The breakfast top seller remains bacon, eggs, hash browns and toast. Lunch's favorites are hamburgers or club sandwich, with ham, turkey and bacon on wonder white toast, with French fries and a cola, and beef, pork, and lamb for dinner. See, diners want meat and potatoes, not fancy vegetable plates and fruit slices. Those items serve as garnish, not substance. High school kids, and I suppose those kids who may go to this new college, don't really eat here unless they are with their families. They'll go to Bob's Burger Shack, or Missy's Malt Shoppe, not here. I suppose they'll have a cafeteria at that college, too, kinda like the high school."

"Yeah, those high school kids kinda like places they don't have to tip."

Nick rested the newspaper in front of Gus as he slid out of the booth. "Gotta get back to the grill, Gussie. Oh, the Hobart jammed again this morning while I was preparing dinner rolls. I'll call Anthony with Elk Grove supplies since he's supposed to service those blades."

Officer Tim O'Hare

Officer Tim O'Hare, of the Grove City Police Department, straddled one of the stainless steel, red vinyl topped stools at the counter. He was cross-examining a plate of burger, fries, and a tall Coke placed before him.

"Excuse me, Teri, could I get another bottle of ketchup, if you've got a minute?"

O'Hare had been with the Grove force for over two years, coming from Mayport County where he began his career.

"Here you go, Sweetie. Heinz okay?"

"So, this new junior college opening down the street, is it gonna cause traffic problems?"

"Yeah, lots of commuting students at that corner. The city is considering installing a traffic light for access to old Route 53. When completed, the college will sit right along that curve."

(At the end of the counter, with his bottom cradling the stool like a limp water balloon, Bob Waylon was considering either the tapioca or rice pudding and coffee. A frequent patron of the Golden Spoon, Bob knew both Teri and Officer O'Hare quite well. Bob drove a bread truck for Wonder and made deliveries here twice a week.)

"Teri, what ya know about that proposed college? What kind of classes are they going to teach? My daughter was going to sign up for that Secretarial School downtown, to learn typing, but man, the price was steep!" Think this new college will teach typing?"

(Bob's daughter Karen works at the Golden Spoon, part-time, to help pay for her car. She's hoping to get on with State Farm as an office secretary but needs to improve her typing skills.)

"Karen's a good little server here, Bob, but she needs to consider her future too. I'm not sure, but maybe that new college will teach business classes, and at a more reasonable cost."

"Don't they teach typing at the high school? Seems some of those kids leave campus early to get work experience. We patrol the high school, and those kids in their souped-up cars go speeding out of the parking lot before the three o'clock release. They say they're going to their work-study job. Caught two drag racing on the frontage road off old Route 53. Sergeant says they watch too many of those 'beach babe' and 'hot rod' movies, think they're James Dean or something. My partner Cliff and I must have ticketed Doc Johnson's kid a half dozen times for one violation or another. He drives that red '65 GTO, hangs out with some blonde kid who runs his '59 Plymouth Fury with loud glass pack mufflers."

"Well, Tim, maybe with the new college and all, some of those kids will consider going to college rather than just hanging around the A&W or the Sunoco gas station admiring their cars. Don't know but kids out of high school gotta find a job if they don't get drafted. Think going to that college will keep them from the draft?"

Chuck Weldone

On the last morning of his life, Chuck Weldone occupied the booth near the south wall featuring the Cézanne still life print of fruit, tablecloth and water pitcher. Never married, Mr. Weldone sat alone, contemplating his plate of fried eggs, hash browns, and acute angled rye toast. Through the near window, he had a view of the horse-collar grill of his teal-colored 1959 Edsel Citation. The vehicle was neatly positioned within two white parking stripes on the east side of the lot. Chuck was proud of his vehicle, and he was one of the first to order it through the dealership in town. His previous car was a large 1952 four-door Lincoln. Chuck liked to drive. He was one of those drivers who just hung on to the wheel while using both feet to brake or accelerate. His vehicle would simply "float" down the road, manned by an occupant who just happened to be in the driver's seat. The top of his balding head and lit cigar were all that was visible through the windshield. The car drove him... he didn't really drive the car.

Chuck is a stout five foot eight, with light complexion and mostly bald. In winter, or when angered, his cheeks redden, making him look very much like Soviet Statesman Nikita Khrushchev. Chuck is not considered an outwardly friendly person. He may even be viewed as somewhat cranky. Many town folks referred to him as an angry George Burns, because he is most often with cigar in hand or mouth and scowling. Kids in his neighborhood often pester him for old cigar boxes they needed for grade school art projects. He rarely accommodates.

Sixty-eight, retired and opinionated, Chuck had fought in WWII (infantry), and he had spent over forty years as a tool and die man. He enjoys eating at the Golden Spoon and does so several times a week. On Wednesdays, he shows up early for the liver and onions dinner special.

Ted Gamble

Looking up from his breakfast plate, Chuck noticed Ted Gamble moving toward his table. (Ted was a fellow member [Korean conflict] of the local VFW Post Chuck often frequented.)

"Hey Chuck, mind if I sit a spell? The wife and I just finished breakfast and now she's chatting with Gloria Seamore about some TV show they've been watching, Peyton Place or something."

"Have a seat, Ted."

A lean and wiry six foot three, Ted could not really fit comfortably in a booth. He sat sideways with his long legs stretched in the isle between Chuck's booth and the empty adjacent table. Ted was an avid bowler and part of two leagues–his church league on Tuesday and the Grove City league on Friday nights. A somewhat aggressive bowler, the spin on his polished sixteen-pound ball was most effective in picking up a 7-10 split.

"I'd rather let the ladies visit without me, and besides, I haven't finished my coffee."

"Speaking about TV, you know I got one of those Curtis Mathes console color TV's. Terrific picture and beautiful color."

(Ted wondered what shows Chuck was watching in color. Maybe Disney on Sunday. Ted knew most shows Chuck was interested in were broadcast in black and white.)

"You've always been the first to buy things with the newest features."

(Ted had heard Chuck boast about the features of his Edsel many times, yet he appreciated his enthusiasm: the pushbutton transmission shifting system in the center of the steering wheel, the rolling-dome speedometer, the low oil level and parking brake warning lights and that big Ford V-8.)

"Say, Chuck, I see they're finally starting work on that college going up down the street."

"Bout time, Ted. Hell, I drive past that large obnoxious plywood sign reading 'Future Site of Grove Junior College' on the curve to old Route 53 every time I leave the restaurant. What 'the devil' is a junior college, anyway? Somehow, the term junior reminds me of junior high school, or junior prom, or junior varsity...a warm-up, an apprenticeship, something that is less than or in preparation for something more permanent."

"Not sure myself, Chuck. As I understand it, anyone can enroll in this college at a really low fee."

"Well, guess who's paying for that! Hell, the town's property taxes already support the area's grade and high schools. Now a junior college! Hope they don't bring in any of those bearded big city war protesting professors. Seen 'em on the news inciting hippie longhair college kids and stirring up draft card burning anti-American activists."

(Oh boy, thought Ted...better find an exit from the old man's tirade. Next, he'll launch into his position on President Johnson and Secretary of Defense McNamara's foreign policy.)

"Not sure that would happen here, but it's nice our high school kids will have another option for college... Well, I'd better get back to my wife's table–supposed to go downtown today. Take 'er easy, Chuck."

Ted noticed Barbara Loftus had joined Gloria Seamore and his wife at the small table where he had left the ladies. Their conversation had moved beyond TV shows. When Ted approached his wife's table, the wholesome homemakers were blushingly discussing their monthly book discussion groups' selection, *The Feminine Mystique*.

"What you ladies reading this month?"

"Oh, a rather enlightening book by Betty Friedan. Alvin Toffler said the book has 'pulled the trigger on history'."

"Who? Are you ready to go, Pat?"

"Just about, I need to freshen up in the ladies' room before we head downtown."

Barbara and Gloria accompanied Pat to the restroom and, along their way, could not miss Gladys Senstrom at a center table.

"Hello, Gladys, saw your picture in today's paper."

"Thank you! We're quite excited that our community will soon have more education options."

"Are you part of a committee for the planned junior college?"

"Well, you know I'm still president of the Grove Women's Club, and I serve on the mayor's City League for Development."

"Yes indeed. Well, gotta run. Good day Gladys."

Inside the restroom, Pat shared her personal experience working with Gladys on the downtown historical beautification project.

"You know the refurbished old train depot? Well, The Historical Society does not recognize it as the 1889 structure. The photos featured in the depot museum clearly display the 1889 design, including the brass plaques etched into the original maple flower boxes. You see, Gladys (the girls often refer to her as 'rubber neck' because of her nosey ease dropping) insisted on replacing the original window flower boxes with newer ones. Myself and the other women on the committee asked Grove's carpenter, Devin Clayborn to refurbish the boxes to original specifications, including polishing the brass-etched plaques! Well, Gladys went ahead and had the original boxes made into window shutters, which were not part of the 1889 design, discarded the brass plaques, and ordered new 'pine' window boxes from Sears."

Gladys Senstrom and Joyce Spellman

Wearing her customary flowered hat, Gladys Senstrom had positioned herself in a center dining area table, beneath the Modigliani print featuring a female with elongated neck.

Today she was sharing a late cup of coffee and thin slice of lemon cake with Joyce Spellman. The two were neighbors in the Elk Heights subdivision. Gladys thought of herself as a "community activist" who was both aware of and involved in local activities. She was essentially a town busybody.

"We're so excited about the new college...did you see our picture in the paper?"

Joyce thought Gladys a bit boastful and full of herself but knew she always had the latest gossip. "Yes indeed, read the article and saw your picture first thing this morning...why weren't you holding the ground-breaking shovel?"

"Oh that. Well the mayor wanted me pictured next to him, between the County Treasurer and the Dean of the College. You know, all of us were provided a special paper written by the original 'junior college' visionaries–William Harper Rainey and J. Stanley Brown at the University of Chicago. Did you know their pilot program, Joliet Junior College, simply served as a grades 13-14 prep school? Our college will not only provide preparation for transfer to four-year college or university but also offer workforce and vocational skills training! That's what some of our kids need. You know, not all high school seniors are 'ready' for real college."

"Are you considering the new junior college for your younger daughter Susan?"

"Oh, nooo, nooo! Susie will follower her sister Sandra and brother Kevin's example and attend the state university here, or an out-of-state select private college. You know my eldest Kevin? Well, just two years out of the university (he was on the Dean's list as a senior), well, the advertising firm where he works, they have promoted him to 'Regional Product Enhancer.' He's in charge of promoting canned Hi-C drinks to all the super markets in Jamestown. And my oldest girl Sandra, you know she studied fashion design at that private northeast liberal arts college, just graduated last June. Oh, you remember, you attended her party at the country club. Well, she's now working in the fashion industry in New York! How exciting!"

(Joyce sensed Gladys's comments were somewhat cutting seeing that her older boy and daughter had not gone away to college. In fact, Joyce's oldest son Calvin worked for a local cement contractor, driving heavy equipment, and he earns a better-than-average salary. He and his wife Loraine were able to buy a big house just north of town. Joyce also knew Gladys' son Kevin's position was nothing more than a low-level sales clerk stocking juice cans on grocery shelves, and her daughter Sandra, who supposedly works in New York's fashion industry, was actually ordering and inventorying bolts of fabric in a warehouse in Queens!)

Jimmy Spellman

Joyce was proud of all her children. Her youngest boy Jimmy was graduating from high school this June, class of 1966. Jimmy certainly has the smarts for college. He has always had a special intellectual curiosity; some call it an artistic, creative and emotionally caring side. He is also ambitious and enterprising.

(Joyce considered the new junior college as an option choice for her son, but not this fall...well, with the tour and all...)

Earlier, during elementary school, young Jimmy would collect and return soda pop empties for coins, and in junior high and early high school delivered the local daily newspaper. Joyce often recalls that her son Jim had been independent and an early age, creative, and introspective.

Once, when on his paper route, Jimmy saw an American Flag displayed at a home where a young man had not returned from service. Having played little league baseball with a boy from that house, he pedaled away on his stingray bike in quiet reverence, considering his own potential draft into America's Southeast Asia conflict.

Jimmy did fairly well in school. Different subjects influenced him in different ways. As a high school junior, he took a yearlong Survey of American Literature class taught by English instructor, Mr. Darren Palmer. Exposure to ideas expressed through the course challenged his thinking, encouraging and influencing his own writing.

Mr. Palmer introduced some challenging themes. Students were asked to explore works of Emerson, Faulkner, Fitzgerald, Salinger, Stein, Thoreau, Twain, Bellow, and Hemmingway. Encouraged by Mr. Palmer, Jim also examined the poetic verse of Whitman, Dickenson, Hughes, Frost, Williams, and Stevens.

(Also employed by Grove City high school, Mr. Palmer's wife Audrey teaches European Art History and directs the drama club. The Palmers rent a colonial house on Driver Street near the country club, where they work part-time during summer break, Darren in the golf clubhouse and Audrey at the tennis shop. Typically seen in white Levis, navy sweaters, and penny loafers, the young and attractive couple share a yellow 1964 Mustang convertible.)

Needing a humanities class as a senior, Jim enrolled in Mrs. Audrey Palmer's European Art History course. Besides, she drove a cool convertible and was "pretty good looking" for a high school teacher. She proved to be a tougher than average grader, requiring weekly check-out and viewing of a number of glossy art books placed on reserve in the library. The course surveyed 15th and 16th century painters, sculptors, and architects. Jim discovered an affection for the lives and works of early Renaissance artists from Italy.

Having a newly acquired interest in art and literature, Jim has recently been expressing himself through writing and music (rock n' roll) with some success.

Two years ago, he saved enough of his paper route coins to order an electric guitar from the *Sears and Roebuck* catalog. A "Silvertone" solid-body six string with amplified speaker built right in the guitar case.

Gladys Senstrom, and most of the adult town folk for that matter, cared little about Joyce's son Jim's musical pursuits, except strangely, one of the Golden Spoon restaurant owners.

Gus Gerinopolis would consistently inquire about Jim and his pals' musical progress. Gus had introduced Jimmy to a terrific young local guitar player, Pastor Dale Foster. Jimmy practiced for more than four months with the Pastor, learning a few cords and the use of the thumb pick. Eight months later, a raucous sound produced through Vox amplifiers, Rickenbacker guitars, Shure microphones, and Ludwig drums echoed from the Spellman's garage.

Just seventeen, Jimmy formed a four-piece band (The Spiders) fashioned after the many "British Invasion" groups i.e., Zombies, Kinks, Gerry and the Pacemakers, Herman's Hermits, and the Dave Clark Five. Accompanying Jimmy were Hoyt Davis (lead singer and rhythm guitar), Stan Hall (bass guitar), and Jay Slowik (drums). The three composed the rhythm section and shared in vocal harmonies. Many thought the length and volume of the group's hair (and sound) outpaced their musicianship, but they had enough talent to cut a record and sign with a local label.

Jamie Cheeto's local recording house helped produce their initial two-sided 45. The recorded track, called "Day's Ease" (music and lyrics by Jimmy and Hoyt) was a play on Jay Gatsby's complex and unstable love relationship with Daisy. The song included some intriguing guitar riffs influenced by guitarists Chuck Berry and Dick Dale. Commercial success was slow. Cheeto sold the rights to that first 45 to Bang records for a small used keyboard and two hundred dollars cash. Bang promoted the 45's flip side titled "Nervous Spider," a parody of a Whitman poem. That song sold nearly twenty thousand copies, placing their band on the charts. The Spiders produced a dozen additional songs with Bang, enough for a whole album.

Their manager, J. Doyle Rozzie, a local musician want-to-be with a Maynard G. Krebs-Dobie Gillis goatee, booked the group in local clubs, dance halls, and as the house band on a local TV station show called Raising-Hits. Just recently however, Rozzie signed The Spiders to tour with the Young Rascals, whose number one hit, "Good Lovin," had sold nearly a million copies. Scheduled for this summer and fall, the tour bills the Spiders as "An Emerging National Act."

Joyce Spellman and husband Clayton signed the contract, enabling Jimmy (being under age 18) to tour through the New England States and Canada. Their manager, Rozzie, has the band dressed in matching dark turtleneck sweaters, slim continental trousers, and Cuban-heeled boots. Jimmy, Hoyt, Stan, and Jay are now preparing for the stage. Their college plans are on hold, for now, and the near future.

Maybe college–junior or otherwise–is not for everyone.

Betty Bueler

Gus's position in the corner booth lends him a clear view of the cash register till drawer. Waitress, hostess, and cash register maiden Betsy Bueler occupies this key position. She also maintains the "books" concerning everything from food costs to laundry service. "Everything okay today, Hon?" can be heard throughout the day as Betsy rings up hand-written figures from paper checks.

With hat and short cigar clenched between his teeth, Chuck Weldone presented cashier Betsy a stained yellow check with cash and coins while grabbing a toothpick and complimentary Sen-Sen mint.

"How were your eggs, Hon?"

"Over-easy, yep, and coffee was warm...this time."

"You should try the lamb chops for dinner this Thursday, Hon."

"Lamb chops? Thought Thursday was meatloaf night."

Looking through the glass case below the cash register counter, Chuck asked the price for the "El Producto Queen Cigar" in the small glass tube... 75 cents!

"Too damn much," he grumbled.

Looking above her bifocal lenses, Betsy expressed a pleasant, "See ya again real soon Hon," as Chuck adjusted the cigar stub nestled between his teeth.

"Yeah, yeah, Betsy, keep the place clean, kiddo."

Heading for the door, Chuck silently tipped his hat after recognizing

Fr. John sitting in the corner booth talking with Gus.

The good Father was soliciting the Golden Spoon to help promote raffle tickets for the St. Jerome's Parish bizarre next month. Fr. John and Gus have what some refer to as a "symbiotic" relationship. The Golden Spoon discounts several thousand pounds of cod each year for the Parish Fish Fry. In exchange, the church bulletin provides free weekly advertising space, promoting The Golden Spoon as the recommended Sunday after-mass breakfast place.

Although Gus and family are Greek Orthodox and members of St. Peter's, Fr. John considers them good "east and west" Catholic friends.

Howard Chive

Aching and empty and not sure why, emeritus university professor Howard Chive wandered to the cigarette machine. Pulling the glass and stainless knob, a fresh pack of Viceroys and paper matchbook dropped in a tray. Packing the tobacco in the palm of his hand, Howard raised a single smoke from the cellophane wrap and struck his Zippo. Inhaling quickly, a puff escaped, and the exhale induced nearly instant satisfaction.

Howard had taught American History at the university for thirty-five years. As emeritus faculty, he visits the campus just a few times a year these days, mostly for some department staff meetings, regional conferences, debates, and commencement. The current dean had asked him whether he would sit on the department's capital development committee. An accomplished academic, Howard maintained a level of antipathy for fundraising. He declined the dean's offer, but he agreed to represent the American History faculty at a scheduled forum this fall.

During his academic career, Howard authored a number of scholarly articles, book chapters, historical publications, and a compendium of Modern American history, designed as supplemental reading for serious graduate students. He enjoys his academic life.

"Well, if it isn't professor Chive. How's Sharon?"

A bit startled from his smoking trance, Howard recognized Bob Waylon.

"Very well, Bob, thanks—and Tracy?"

"Yes, she's terrific, still at Campton Elementary, likes the new principal too."

Bob reached for change from his pocket and fed the cigarette machine. A soft pack of Tareyton smokes appeared with matchbook. Then the crunch of cellophane helped expose a cig. Cupping his large hands around a small paper match, Bob lit up.

The two smoking men proceeded slowly toward the small booth Howard had occupied.

"What do you 'up-state' university folk think about the new college here?"

"Well, I'm not really that familiar with such institutions. Even so, the expansion and diversity of educational offerings are emblematic of our country's development. Jefferson and our idealistic forefathers may have envisioned such evolution."

"I did read about a year or so ago, in an editorial piece in the student newspaper, *Lancet,* something about the junior college. I believe some teacher college students had posed a number of concerns, in the form of questions, for undergraduate response. Some notion of the college's purpose. The uniqueness of a two-year, open-admission college's transitional motive. An institution that serves, or is perceived to serve, as an equalizer to better 'democratize' higher education. Whether the behavior and practice of such institutions mimic the secondary school experience, and if they aspire to have equal reputations and legacies as four-year colleges and universities. I recall Felix E. Schelling stating that 'true education makes for inequality; the inequality of individuality, the inequality of success; the glorious inequality of talent; of genius; for inequality, not mediocrity, individual superiority, not standardization is the measure of the progress of the world.' But I'm uncertain of the Junior College's intended purpose beyond providing access to a level of higher education study."

"So, do you think this junior college will fit well here in Grove City?"

"Not certain how this college will be perceived through the eyes of their elementary and high school contemporaries, whether a convivial relationship will aspire. These systems have parent/teacher conferences, geographically local school boards, and neighborhood schools. The junior college institutions appear to operate as a grade 13-14 'middle position' following secondary education and preceding university sponsored higher education. I guess from a university perspective, such 'junior colleges' are euphemistically referred as a 'technical institutions' or 'trade colleges.' A college education, and in a sense all education, cannot really be prepackaged. One may suppose working with students in the first two years of their higher education experience-whether their goals are vocational or academic, should offer, maintain, and promote a free exchange of ideas..."

Suddenly, interrupting the two men's conversation, was the commotion of Officer Tim O'Hare scurrying through the front entrance, trailed closely by Fr. John, reacting to what appeared to be an urgent police call.

A bustle of restaurant patrons, led by Gladys Senstrom, began moving towards the front entrance.

Exiting the women's restroom, Ted Gamble's wife Pat and accompanying friends Gloria and Barbara Loftus noticed Ted clamoring near a window as Officer O'Hare and Fr. John sped off in the lights flashing-patrol car. Joyce Spellman moved toward the lunch counter where server Teri was peering over her glasses as she wiped her hands on her apron. "What the hell's going on?"

Teri moved more deliberately toward the commotion, passing Howard and Bob, who had snuffed out their cigarettes and were now standing outside their booth.

Nick, hearing the clatter through the aluminum kitchen door, joined the audience in his chef cap and apron.

"What the hell's going on?" Teri repeated.

Making his way from the parking lot, a panting Jack Reardon loudly affirmed:

"There was a huge accident out near old Route 53, just past the curve! Several vehicles, one's flipped upside down, looks to be fatalities."

Ted Gamble's height advantage enabled him to see over the crowd forming near the outside window. "There's smoke out west near the frontage road, fire too."

By now, Gladys Senstrom had made it to her '63 Chevy Biscayne and was boarding the vehicle. As she sped off in the direction of the smoke, a wind gust removed her flowered hat, exposing her disheveled red hair.

"That's a dangerous curve up there," repeated Bob Waylon. "Kids like drag racing on that frontage road. Maybe one of 'em missed the curve."

"Reardon thinks the flipped car was light green, and a motorbike might be in the mix."

"Hey, old man Weldone drives a teal Edsel. He just left here about twenty minutes ago."

Ted Gamble had left Pat at the restaurant—he was in his truck heading toward the accident scene. He was just trying to figure out how bad it was.

Joyce Spellman was clutching her purse and chatting with professor Chive. "Hope no one's too seriously hurt. The city is supposed to place a traffic light near that curve, especially with the college going up there."

"It would certainly be a shame. Seems automobiles kill or injure more citizens each year."

Howard lit another smoke and gazed out the window towards his silver Buick.

"Some police activity just outside the restaurant, setting up a detour or something. We may need to avoid old Route 53 and the accident scene altogether."

Two squad cars had positioned themselves to direct restaurant traffic to exit eastbound only. The police hoped to stop any vehicle movement towards the accident area. One officer approached the front entrance.

"Hello folks, I'm Officer Pagonski. On your way out, you'll need to exit east due to an accident closing access to the frontage road and old Route 53."

"What the hell's going on with the crash?" exclaimed Teri.

"Can't tell you too much other than it's a mess. Involves four cars and a motorbike; well, not really. The motorbike is a witness. This kid on a Cushman scooter said he saw the whole thing. A maroon Corvair was chasing some red Pontiac GTO north bound on frontage road, and they were unable to navigate the old Route 53 curve. One guy's dead. A Plymouth, trying to pass a car southbound on the curve, forced an older model Edsel off the road. Plowed right into that big plywood sign for the new college site. Car flipped several times, landed upside down. Guy still had a lit cigar in his mouth when they dragged him out. Priest was there to administer last rights. Sad, really... Oh, and the sign reading 'Future Site of Grove Junior College' burnt up and burst into pieces, smoldering pieces of plywood everywhere, not a real good start for the college...don't know much else...just exit the restaurant parking lot eastbound only."

Throughout all the raucous and commotion, Gus remained seated in the corner booth, nearest the cash register. He had a clear view of the cash till drawer, where cashier Betsy Bueler maintained her post.

Gus tapped his filtered cig on the glass amber ashtray-- quietly humming J.S. Bach's Brandenburg Concerto No. 5.

Community Colleges: Exporting Middle Class Dreams

By Jann M. Contento and Jeffrey Ross

Copperfield Publishing, LTD. (An Arizona Corporation)

Many countries are currently considering diversifying their higher education systems by modeling U.S. community college-like institutional designs.

Vietnam and China, along with other nations, are intrigued, curio us, yet somewhat suspicious of American community colleges–especially in terms of their relationship to universities and higher learning.

How can one distinguish the cultural differences, in general, between community colleges and universities? Certainly, one could consider faculty credentials, administrative staff preparation, academics, service focus, student "learning readiness," institutional missions, vocational training–the obvious and usual. Community colleges do an ample job of preparing students for the next steps in their lives. They provide a valuable entry point for a richer participation in American society–and can potentially accelerate a student's quality of life, both on the job and in the soul.

However, we believe there is a fundamental divergence in the culture of the community college which has to do with a social or class distinction criterion–we believe that community colleges aspire to prepare their students for entry *into* the middle class, while universities have aspired to pull their students *out* of the middle class. We are not economists, political scientists, nor sociologists. We are simply steady observers of community college riffs and phrasings...

An examination of "class" differentiation mechanisms at American community colleges provides relevant insights about American value systems–and the desperate conformity magnified and then embraced by so many.

The dialectal response to community "middle class" composite cultural needs, economic needs, training needs–and response to university adjustments in academic articulation matters–keeps the community colleges flexible and "organically" (as in 19th century romantic philosophy) reactive.

Community colleges, we believe, have become the protectors of the American middles (We have borrowed the contextual use of this term from the American novelist John Updike). Although not consciously intended, community colleges have evolved into places of great tension–tension between developmental (remediation), academic and vocational/occupational demands, tension between traditional (face-to-face) and online course offerings–and tension among local "stakeholders" concerning staff salaries, travel expenses, baccalaureate training, and bond elections.

The hopeful middles at the community college, our students, struggle to obtain training, to prepare for further schooling, to live and to love.

The emergence of "work force development," supported by ancillary academic programs, appears to be the actual driving force behind community college post-secondary education "market share" positioning. Is this altogether bad? Poverty is not good. Yet, our notions of the middle class have both material and intellectual undertones.

We sense that 21st century middle class America cares far more about their material well-being than their intellectual or humanistic pelf.

Surely, the American middle class is becoming more expansive in its demands for goods and services. Think of the size, configuration, amenities and prestige of today's modern American home. The trickle upward of buying power and the all-encompassing "religion of stuff" appears to be thriving–no matter what one thinks about the economic situation. Available "work" and accelerating salaries have driven the economy.

The idea of the community college (a priori) was certainly poetic, certainly beautiful, a metaphor for entrance into prosperous–and informed– American middle life. The post WW II individual American experience has centered on the development of a (seemingly) nourished and materially satiated middle class. What do English Language Learning (ELL) training, General Educational Development (GED) training, and massage therapy training have in common? They are all entry point activities to a better "quality" of life.

However, most of the "stuff" Americans harbor in their homes and hearts has done little to improve the "core" quality of lives. The entire middles-desired "standard of living" system is showing signs of near collapse in respect to current economic conditions (i.e., mortgage default rates, banking industry regulations, automobile industry failures, and credit card restructuring laws). What would one do without streaming videos and smartphones? (Save money, think, and reflect more? Foster altruism?)

The middle class is a fertile ground for illusions–big dreams and big payments–a life of "gilded" servitude, a standard of living that promises much but struggles to deliver a wholesome future.

Ah, but for all classes the middle endgame is perhaps, well, a dreamscape.

One can take this axiom to the "proverbial" bank: the more things one possesses, the more one is possessed by those things. Sadly, the middle's intellect seems to be now vigorously centering on Disneyland fantasies and happy hours (where the "middle" really expands). The creation and maintenance of a standard of living, and making a living, is not mysterious.

Economists have carefully studied the relationships between behavior and the economy. The institutionalist school of economics, for example, sees behavior as part of a larger social pattern influenced by current ways of living and modes of thought. But knowing *how* to live may be the greatest secret of all.

Wealth without sensitivity, without reflection, without conscience, creates a kind of tyranny in personal, domestic, and global understanding. What should the middles' intellectual values reflect? How should vocational, avocational, and intellectual meaning offered by American community colleges trisect for the ambiguous middles? How often do community college instructors hear the phrase, "Oh, I'm just taking these classes (English, math, history–insert name of academic courses) to get them out of the way"? Many may nod in gentle agreement, empathetic to the view that coursework of any kind is simply preparation for the world of work and ownership–a rite of passage into the middles. The place where many of us may, too, live and function...

During the last fifteen years, the (at-times) repressive nature of corporate management models at the community colleges has, perhaps, changed the relationships between students and staff. Certainly, college staff (especially faculty and administration) depends on student enrollment (and fees) to support their own enhanced middle class aspirations. We are not hinting at class exploitation so much as we are describing an emerging truth in the community college formula; faculty and administrators have developed a symbiotic relationship with students.

The students' success stories advertently elevate employee status (and incomes) by helping more students INTO the middle class, administrators and faculty may—by virtue of their actions—be elevating themselves OUT of the middles.

Even so—those of us who work in academic disciplines at the community colleges should continue our most important task: promoting how to live and how to improve the quality of the intellectual life—not just how to make a living. Poverty of spirit, we believe, is the worst kind of destitude.

What will the newly emerging international models of the community college emphasize? What capitalist and corporate accouterments will they convey? How will these institutions improve the quality of their students' lives?

It may be time to rethink the idiomatic daydreams we create in the middles and in "middle" education...

This article by Jeffrey Ross and Jann M. Contento was originally printed in *Academic Leader*, VOLUME 26, NUMBER 6 JUNE 2010.

@ Tri-Campus Central College

By David Forrester, actual ENG 101 student–not an Actor

I remember the first day I walked into Dr Roz's ENG 101 class. For a number of years, I hadn't been out in society very much, and I was immediately put at ease by the laid-back atmosphere in the classroom. As the room began to fill up with students, I observed that outside of one lady, I looked to be the oldest student there. At first, I felt a bit self-conscious, but Dr Roz's dry sense of humor and mild manner was very easy to warm up to. I instinctively knew that this was going to be a safe place. It might even be a place that I could enjoy coming to, and I could learn more about the subject of writing which I loved so much.

It didn't take long for me to be keenly aware of the fact that Dr Roz was a master of his trade. Learning consistently the amazing strategies of putting together a meaningful composition that stated clearly, exactly what I was trying to articulate, was intriguing. As time went on, I found myself gaining a certain confidence, not only concerning writing, but also, maybe even more importantly, feeling more comfortable sharing my ideas with other people and listening to how they were experiencing the class. I knew this was an important and significant chapter in my life, and I felt a deepening sense of gratitude for the way Dr Roz personalized the class and, at the same time, instructed us with an undeniable mastery. I thoroughly enjoyed my community college experience at good old Tri-Campus.

@ Copperfield High School–Home of the Copperheads

By Dr. John Paddison

To make time pass more swiftly, Joel inspected closely the boring sameness of the classroom, a mirror of the many others he had endured during his past three years at Copperfield High School–Home of the Copperheads. The barrenness of the four faded, utility-white walls, the stolid dullness of the teachers, the banks of windows looking out into the sliver of sky beyond the other neighboring bank of classroom windows. The white chalk dust and black chalkboards. The work-covered teacher desk prominently positioned in the center front of the classroom, monitoring all the subservient rows of smaller student desks. The stiff cork bulletin boards containing nothing but last semester's schedule of the Steeler's football team and maybe a tattered purple Copperfield High School Booster Club ribbon and perhaps a yellowed newspaper article about the teacher's subject matter.

The recurring scene seemed to him to be one coming straight out of a T. S. Elliot work, a graphic representation of the poet's imagery of desolation and desperation too often representative of the human experience. Mr. Bivens had read "The Love Song of J. Alfred Prufrock," first softly and then again with vigor in the literature class he had just come from, the only one he truly enjoyed and looked forward to attending on Tuesday and Thursday mornings. Mr. Bivens' respect for and love of poetry, and obviously language and literature–for knowledge and learning in general–added to the poem's challenging, amusing obscurity. Bivens' homework assignment was to critically read "The Wasteland" so the students could discuss the broader social implications during the next class.

Having previously read the work several times, and marveling at the author's artful, powerfully poignant way of portraying life's disillusionment, Joel remained certain that he could bring up the sterility of classrooms as a relevant example of the bleakness of current educational forms. Elliot's persona had described Joel's premise exactly, so he had underlined the passage: "And I have known the eyes already, known them all–/The eyes that fix you in a formulated phrase,/And when I am formulated, sprawling on a pin,/When I am pinned and wriggling on the wall,/Then how should I begin/To spit out all the butt-ends of my days and ways?/" Now immersed in his own empty environs, Joel relished the rich evocativeness of those particular stanzas from Prufrock.

Like his peers sitting around him, Joel slouched down deeply in the uncomfortable wooden chair/desk, hoping to remain unnoticed and thus un-interrogated. He stared at the ducktail on the back of Jack Reynolds' head, immediate in front of him. He knew Reynolds probably amused himself by making lurid gestures to Sandy Martin, who sat smiling coyly back at Jack through the open door of her algebra class, diagonally across the empty hall. Her fat fingers gently massaged the crucifix hanging down on her blue fuzzy sweater.

At the front of the class, Mr. Ames droned on about the three branches of federal government, diagramming them artfully on the blackboard and connecting them with back and forth arrows of clarification. The skinny, dour civics teacher looked like an undertaker or a conjurer. A receding hairline had cleared the entire crown of his head, so he combed his remaining hair slicked back around the sides and down the back of his head. The boys in the back of the classroom laughingly called it the "fire path" hairstyle.

The class listened passively, subserviently, especially the group who was not on the college track—those who never sat in the front row of desks. Ames prided himself on belittling the rabble in the rear of the room— the "dirtyneckers" he called them in the faculty break room. The lassitude of those students came, no doubt, from either indifference or more probably from Ames' reputation as a "hard ass."

For example, a few weeks prior, Ralph Dummund, who sat in the last row, asked Ames, not in a smart-ass way or anything, for a point of clarification about the role of the vice-president in government. Above the tight collar of his white shirt and wide black tie, Ames' narrow face reddened with exasperation, suddenly transforming its pale pastiness, and the vein in his forehead throbbed beneath the thin patch of hair surrounding his shiny bald head.

"Don't you people back here ever read?" Ames asked deliberately as he walked back and stood before Ralph's desk. "Mr. Dumbdumb...oh, I mean Mr. Dummund," he began and then paused so his response would have maximum effect. "The answer to your question is on page 181 in the textbook!"

The irritated teacher continued in a slow, sarcastic tone. "If you had done the reading, sir, you would know the answer to your own inane question and would not have to waste precious class time with your disruptive antics!" Aims certainly had a way with words. After a smattering of low laughs and phony coughs came from those in the front rows, Ames returned triumphantly to his podium and resumed the lecture. During the rest of the class session, no further questions came from Ralph or from the any of the others in the rear of the room. In fact, the poignant and stinging incident produced a silence in the back of the room that would undoubtedly last for the remainder of the semester.

Watching the insanely slow clock hanging high above Ames' talking head, Joel waited patiently for class to end. Then lunch. Then gym class, with its never-ending embarrassment. Then mechanical arts, then auto shop, and finally freedom.

He carefully chanced a glance over at Lindsey Childress' long brown hair flowing smoothly down over her shoulders and at the maturing beauty of her facial profile and her super-fine legs.

He still loved Lindsey but had long since conceded his unworthiness. Lindsey just sat at her desk, her heavily lip-sticked red lips pursed contentedly as she wistfully watched out the window, her fingers absently, dreamily, curling the tips of a full strand of her beautiful hair. Lindsey, along with Stodemeyer, had been crowned the homecoming royalty the past fall and now students idolized the matched set of charmingly attractive people. Stodemeyer, the handsome, privileged jock who once during gym class had rubbed a damp athletic supporter in Herman Wilson's face. Mr. Monahan, the senior gym teacher, as well as the Copperfield's head football coach, just laughed at the young athlete's antics. He wished he had a cool-sounding family name like Stodemeyer...or Mondragon, the senior class president... anything but dumb Sheppard.

The 11:30 bell rang, jerking Joel back into the narrowness of his reality. He got up and hurried out into the sickening smell emanating from Mrs. McGuinness' biology class and permeating the hallway. To Mrs.

McG's waddling delight, the shipment of formaldehyde-preserved lab cats used for her advanced biology dissection class had arrived, stinking the whole building up all the way to both exits. Moving quickly through the crowded hallway, Joel stuffed his books into his locker and grabbed his sack lunch, all the while holding his breath until finally emerging from the south exit, out into the bright sunlight and freedom of the early spring afternoon. Finally outside, but still smelling the strong odor of the embalming fluid, he gasped for air several times.

Mrs. McGuinness, like the rest of the faculty, had her own unique method of transforming students into knowledgeable adults...or maybe of imposing her unique form of Prufrockian drudgery onto them. Just like Mrs. Etherton, who drilled her students hard so they could become one with their Royal typewriters. To accomplish this Zen-like state, her monotonous drills required the students, hunched over their machines, to type numerous repetitions of "The quick brown fox jumped over the lazy red hen," done over and over again to the tune of eight-count military marches played scratchily on an old 78 record player. She prowled the rows as the students worked, holding a stop watch suspended from a lanyard hanging around her neck. Or ancient Mr. Banks, the history teacher who stood immutable behind his podium, positioned front dead center in the classroom, reading in monotone from his notes, turning each used and yellowed sheet of American history facts...page after page until the hour of class time ended...timing his lecture so it concluded at the exact moment the dismissal bell sounded, at which point he would mechanically announce, "Test on Friday! Come Prepared!"

All the Copperfield High pedants seemed possessed by no higher passion than to instruct and then go home, and to somehow survive another semester. They, like J. Alfred, used their tiny coffee spoons of ability to monotonously measure out lives of quiet desperation.

Feeling as though he was invisible, Joel made his way through the crowds of underclassmen to the relative quiet of the senior quad and sat down alone on the soft grass. All his former friends had dropped out of school and moved on with their lives, becoming laborer apprentices or pizza delivery men or other such endeavors. Joel's association with them early on in his high school career caused him to be pretty much lumped in with the "ne'er do wells" and "freams" and "no accounts."

Consequently, his counselor, Mr. Lawrence Hightower, recognizing his young advisee's innate lack of potential, wisely steered Joel into the "technical training" track–that narrow, specific curriculum designed to prepare students for attendance at Copperfield Community College. Or perhaps employment at one of the ancillary industries supporting local copper mining.

He could well be trained to use his hands instead of his mind. Hightower grudgingly enrolled him in the few mandatory courses required for graduation, and allowed him a few Spanish classes, but the remainder of his studies were devoted to turning him into a proficient, pliable worker. Regularly each semester Joel found himself in metal shop or wood shop or mechanics or one of the various "hands on" courses requiring little intellectual engagement or higher order thinking skills. But the courses remained consistently easy, so Joel didn't mind being consigned to the path of least resistance. After all, most of the people he knew were regularly enrolled in those "job training" courses as well.

In his last year of schooling, his acquaintances had become almost non-existent. A couple of the others from the neighborhood–even ol' Chucky D.–currently sat in juvenile detention for various petty crimes. Others had lucrative jobs as dishwashers or construction helpers. So, Joel knew very few of those around him–those whose names appeared repeatedly in *The Copperhead Review*, the school newspaper, or those who were listed on the playbills of the drama club's ever-popular productions.

But he had somehow not dropped out...had achieved the rank of senior and as such could freely roam the senior quad unchallenged, though he did often get questioning looks from the college-bound students who walked past him. He never actually felt cheated, though. Just wanted to not stand out and to be quit of the oppressive educational system as quickly as possible. He would soon be the first ever in his family to finish school and graduate. And he planned to leave immediately after graduation and join the army. Maybe become an infantryman or a paratrooper and be a hero like his old man.

Yet there had been somewhat of an anomaly in his final year at Copperfield High. During his last semester, instead of being assigned to the final course in the "Bonehead English" series, Remedial Writing, which involved a semester of creating meaningless sentences and paragraphs with no context, he had somehow mistakenly been placed into Wendell Biven's college-preparatory Advance Placement Literature class. Because he had read most of the books on the reading list Bivens handed out during the first class, Joel said nothing about the mistaken placement and completed all of the coursework with little difficulty. He figured by doing so, he would have the last laugh on his patronizing counselor, Mr. Hightower.

Mr. Bivens was a low-key, nondescript, contemplative sort of guy–middle-aged, with streaks of gray tracing through his brown hair. He taught by continually asking students for their opinions and ideas as though he genuinely cared what they thought and said and related their ideas to the subject matter. He approached them with an air of quiet self-assurance tempered by an equal measure of humility. The young, college-bound school girls flushed innocently when he asked the class pointed, evocative, thought-provoking questions about the texts they read. The boys, too, were quite taken with his teaching style and looked on him as some sort of a father figure, only in a respectful kind of way. But without doubt, his students looked forward to attending his class, enjoying the openness of his "forum for critical awareness and inquiry," as he called his classroom.

That afternoon, after Mr. Hicks' auto mechanics class, Joel walked in from the shop facilities, which lay far out on the fringe of the main campus, and went over to the language arts building. For some reason, he passed slowly by Mr. Bivens' classroom and cautiously peered in. After going back and forth by the door a few more time, he decided to enter and speak with the teacher. After all, Bivens had written a note at the bottom of Joel's last essay about James Joyce's "Araby" being a story about people's crippling suppression of their emotions, saying "I am very impressed with the depth of your ideas. I would like to talk with you sometime regarding the quality of your writing and insights."

Standing in the rear of the classroom, Bivens had his back turned towards Joel. As he always did, the teacher was putting some nonsense riddle or paradox or philosophical saying on the bulletin board for the students to ponder during the next day's classes. Joel shifted his weight from one foot to the other then finally cleared his throat.

Bivens turned around and smiled as soon as he saw Joel. "Oh. Hi, there. I didn't see you come in." Immediately sensing the young man's uneasiness, the teacher motioned him to a desk and sat down across from him. "It's Joel, right?"

"Yeah. Joel Sheppard." They sat for a while in awkward silence then Joel took the essay from his pocket, unfolded it slowly, and passed it to the teacher.

Bivens scanned the essay for a few minutes and then said, "Yes...yes, I remember this. I was really taken with your understanding of Joyce's theme in the story."

Joel could only hunch over and look nervously at the paper. No one had ever said such a thing to him. "Thanks for not squealing on me about being mis-assigned to your honors class...about me not belonging in advanced placement and all."

"Oh, you belong here, all right. No doubt about that! I was surprised, though, that I hadn't seen you in the Honors Program before." After a few moments of thoughtfully watching the young student, Bivens asked, "You're graduating after this semester, aren't you? What are you going to do?"

"I don't know. My counselor says I should go on to Copperfield Community College...or maybe join the army."

"What've you decided?"

"I dunno... I heard some of the teachers here talking. They said Copperfield Community isn't really college...it's like grades 13 and 14...and the only people that teach there are not smart enough to teach at a university. That leaves the army, I guess. Nothing else to do. I don't want to work in the mines like my old man."

"How about a four-year college or a university?"

"College? Naw, I'm not going. I don't have the grades...never took the right classes, either."

"What a shame."

"Huh?"

"Seems as though you've been cheated somewhere along the way– grandly swindled, actually. You really should be considering going on with your education. Not to would be such a waste. Who is your guidance counselor? Lawrence Hightower, I suspect."

"Yeah, him. I don't like him much."

"No. I don't either."

Bivens continued studying Joel intently... not in an intimidating way, but rather with a good deal of interest... as though he actually cared about the young man's future.

"Now, how can I help you?"

"You're not like the other moldies here," Joel finally managed. "I mean, you seem...I don't know...to care about kids...like, if they learn and stuff."

"Yes, I do. Very much so."

"How come you teach?"

"I don't know. Because of a guy named Ralph Waldo Emerson, I guess. He taught me young people are a truly special breed. Looking at you, sitting across from me now, I see you as Truth's longing for itself. Emerson called the phenomena Man Thinking...'the sound estate of all.' That's what makes students all so special. Especially those like you."

"I ain't so special. I know plenty of kids like me. We ain't so special."

"But you are. All of you. You have only to embrace the notion of your uniqueness...to find and explore and embrace the potential within you."

"How's that?" Joel asked, not really understanding but not wanting to sound like a smart aleck.

"Tough to explain. The best way I can describe it is that somehow or another, through the various processes of your life, you–and too many others like you, really–have had the 'Yes, but...' stolen from you. By people like Hightower. And many others, for that matter."

"The what?"

"The 'Yes, but...'." Bivens paused for a moment, collecting his thoughts. "Remember seeing little kids? How they are continuously asking questions? 'What's this?' How's this work?' Why's this happening?' Their very existence is driven by an innate curiosity about the world. But somehow or another the education system, along with other cultural and social forces as well, eventually squelch that basic sense of wonder and excitement right out of them. Thoroughly...systematically...almost completely in too many cases!"

Joel wasn't sure of what to say, so Bivens continued.

"It's the sense of critical awareness all people inherently possess. That's what's taken away. Stealthily stolen from you without your even knowing. Look at it like this. When someone tells you something, you are no longer willing or able or want to look at him or her straight in the eye and say, 'Yes, but what about such and such...?' and really yearn to know the answer, especially concerning life's vital questions about human justice and purpose and responsibility."

The memory of poor Ralph Dummond's humiliation by Ames earlier in the semester flashed into his mind. "Yeah. I kinda dig what you're saying...what you mean. At least I think I do."

"You're an intelligent young man. You shouldn't let anyone or anything convince you otherwise. Continually interrogate the unanalyzed assumptions you've acquired about the world around you...always examine closely your preconceived notions of your existence. Constantly ask how they came about and if they are valid and if not, why not. Give intense scrutiny to who and what these often-erroneous beliefs represent and why."

The weightiness of the talk seemed to overwhelm them, leaving both at a loss for words, so the two sat for a few moments before the awkward silence became unbearable. Perhaps sensing he had inadvertently ventured into an area he had never been before, Joel picked up his paper, rose up and prepared to go.

"Thanks for talking with me, Mr. Bivens. I gotta go now," Joel said, and he turned towards the classroom door.

Before he could leave, however, Mr. Bivens stopped him. Going over to the bookcase of hardcover classics he leant out or sometimes just gave to his students, he stopped and searched the rows until he found the particular volume he wanted. He reached up and took down a heavily dog-eared copy of *The American Scholar and Other Essays by Ralph Waldo Emerson.*

"Here. I think you might truly enjoy this," Bivens said as he handed the volume to Joel. "Read some of it if you have the time. Especially 'The American Scholar.' Stop by again and we'll talk some more. I'd be interested to hear what you think about Emerson's ideas."

When Joel left the teacher's classroom that afternoon, he felt a strange sense of exhilaration...of insipient understanding...a good uneasiness he savored pleasantly. Nobody...no adult...had given him that much attention...not even Mrs. Phelps. Later that night, as he perused the heady book, he regretted not having enough nerve to have talked longer with the teacher.

In the class discussions following that afternoon talk, Mr. Bivens paid no special mind to him, treating Joel as he always had since the beginning of the class...responding to him like he did all the other students...as an intelligent young being...asking him difficult questions and caroming his responses off the other students...as though he, like the others, had insightful, even important things to say.

And during the next several days Joel read and reread "The Scholar" earnestly, making notes and carefully looking up unclear words and obscure references. His light class load afforded him much time to do so. After getting a rudimentary understanding of Emerson's premises, Joel stopped by Bivens' desk after class one day and asked if he could come by and see him that afternoon, to which the teacher smiled widely and nodded his approval. "Sure! Come on by!"

After leaving his auto shop class, Joel once more approached Bivens' classroom, but again with somewhat of a degree of trepidation. He wondered if perhaps the whole thing had been a hoax and the final joke might be on him. What if the teacher had gathered the entire honors class there in order to expose Joel as a fake? Laugh at him and all. Reveal the young man to be the fraud he really was. But when he entered the quiet classroom, the only person there was Bivens, who just sat at his desk, his head bent down as he read student papers.

As Joel entered, the two exchanged pleasantries, and Bivens invited Joel to sit down in the chair beside the desk.

"What's on your mind?"

"Here's your book...*Emerson's essays*." After a bit of hesitation, Joel went on. "I'm kinda wonderin'. Why'd you give it to me?"

"Thought you would appreciate it...maybe find some relevance in Emerson's ideas about throwing off old, oppressive forms in order to find a new self. Did you enjoy it?

"Yeah. I guess. Kinda hard to understand, but interesting."

"You remember the other day when you stopped by and we talked, you asked me why I taught." He paused for a long moment before continuing, leaning back in his chair and putting his hands behind his head. Thinking his ideas through and carefully choosing his words, he went on. "The question bothered me for several hours. For several days, even. Still does, a bit."

"I didn't mean no disrespect."

"No, no, I know that. I'm glad you asked that question because it represents the honest critical inquiry we talked about when you and I la st met. And the question also reminded me of something."

Bivens again hesitated briefly, gathering his thoughts, weighting how best to convey them to the young man. Then he leaned forward and continued.

"When I became a teacher, I promised myself to always remember and thus reassess the reasons why I teach. Doing so, I thought, would always keep my teaching alive and relevant. But somehow over the years I have stopped doing that. I have passively, unconsciously become drawn into a false sense of self-importance. That is, I have, over the years allowed myself to be gradually lured into a narrow sliver of a world where overwhelming small-mindedness numbs and eventually suffocates the human spirit. Seems as though I have gradually become more and more blinded to seeing the broader horizons of promises fulfilled."

Bivens looked directly at his young student before speaking again.

"Your question, though, brought back to my mind Emerson's ideas in 'The American Scholar'. He said something to the effect that many teachers try so hard to educate students but too often c ome up short. They cut up the kindling of knowledge and carefully stack it into a neat pyre-like pile. But they somehow fail to spark the fire that ignites and reinvents and recreates the young imagination...that kindles the passion of and for being human...those forces which illuminate and thus liberate the soul. The Soul Active, he called it. Every day, looking all around this campus, I see those forces lying dormant in so many young people. And I feel so powerless. I realize now that I have unconsciously allowed myself to capitulate to the oppressiveness of broader cultural and social influences. And I now understand I must recommit myself to those universal, transcendent principles and universal processes I discovered long ago."

Bivens stopped once more to again regroup his thoughts and asked almost secretively. "Do you know what alchemy is?"

"Yeah...kinda. It's from olden times, isn't it? When wizards or chemists or something tried to turn common, worthless stuff into gold."

"Yes, but the concept is much more metaphysical. I think of teaching as alchemy and teachers as alchemists. Only in a metaphoric way. You see, teaching is the science of constantly looking for that rare quicksilver moment when one can enable and thus witness the transformation of a young mind into a creative, critical entity. To me that is the gold. And the process is what fascinates me most...finding and using the philosopher's stone reputed to be the magical element...the mysterious catalyst for what Emerson called the 'the transmuting of life into truth'."

After several moments of looking off into nowhere, he turned back towards Joel.

Joel spoke softly. "But I don't understand. How's alchemy related to me? And other nothing guys like me?"

"Emerson's premise is simply anyone...everyone...can be a genius. Even the farmer out in his fields, walking steadily behind his horse and the shiny plow as it turns up the rich earth. The Soul Active. He maintains that every person in the world has the innate quality, the instinctive ability of questioning his or her circumstances–that is, the process of critical inquiry that seeks truth and from this truth creates knowledge and awareness of the world. Gaining knowledge and awareness allows the individual to proactively, creatively, honestly respond to his or her circumstances and existence, to act with justice and responsibility rather than being continually acted upon. Unfortunately, this inborn quality remains dormant and often suppressed in most people. And I guess that is what I see happening in you, Joel."

"In what way?"

"You, like so many of people, myself included, gradually, subtly fall victim to the lies and distortions we have been relentlessly told, about ourselves, about other people—misrepresentations of and about the world around us. Yet these illusions of the past must be continually and closely interrogated and those found to destructive must be thrown off by the truths embedded in the future–life's 'gold,' waiting to be brought forth to achieve the purity of human experience."

Joel laughed a bit, perhaps in uneasiness, maybe in understanding. "Yeah. I guess that's what Emerson meant when he said that mankind was created with eyes in the front of the head and not the back. So, people can look to what's ahead and not behind. You know, learn from those things without being a slave to them, I guess."

Bivens laughed, too, quite delighted by the perception and humanness of the young student. "Yes, I do believe that's what he meant! Precisely!"

The two just looked at each other. Somehow a bond of friendship had been formed between them. Finally, Bivens spoke softly. "Sorry, I'm talking your ear off."

"Naw, I dig what you're saying, man. It's just..." Joel sat silent for a few moments, swallowing hard several times. Out of habit, he tried to keep himself from showing too much emotion and thus appearing vulnerable, but he was unsuccessful as his voice broke a few times. "It's just that I haven't ever...had anyone talk with me like this...had anyone tell me things like this before."

"It's been my pleasure. You are a very intelligent young man. And thanks for reminding me of my original purpose for teaching; to always strive to be a catalyst of sorts for young people like yourself."

"Yeah, like some kinda alchemist, maybe."

Bivens smiled and placed his hand on Joel's shoulder. "I know you will prevail."

With that Joel and Bivens both stood up. "Thanks, man. See ya," Joel said and then went on his way.

Several times before his graduation Joel stopped by to see Mr. Bivens and discuss Emerson, or Holden Caulfield and what being a "catcher in the rye" involved, or other things literary, or just to talk. Bivens did his best to try and help Joel search for various colleges he might attend and apply to for scholarship support.

But in the end, however, the young man's enthusiasm for any such plans dwindled. The siren song of Copperfield seemed to have been etched too deeply into his soul.

On the last day of class, Bivens stopped Joel as he left the classroom. He shook the young man's hand in congratulations then handed him a new copy of Emerson's essay collection. Later, as Joel walked for the last time down the hallway, down by Mr. Ames empty, silent classroom, down by the lingering trace smell of formaldehyde, he opened the book to a page held by the placement of a stiff, new bookmark. An underlined passage, done no doubt by Bivens, seemed to speak directed to him: "For the ease and pleasure of trending the old road, accepting the fashions, the education, the religion of society, he takes the cross of making his own, and, of course, the self-accusation, the faint heart, the frequent uncertainty and loss of time, which are the nettles and tangling vines in the way of the self-relying and self-directed; and the state of virtual hostility in which he seems to stand to society, and especially to educated society." Beside the passage the teacher had also written: "Remember that the essence of your existence is and always will be that of philosopher's stone! W. Bivens."

Joel closed the book and moved on. Shortly after graduation, he enrolled in the fall semester of Copperfield Community College. But because of his high draft number, he was soon taken into the U.S. Army, went to Fort Ord for basic training, then to Fort Leonard Wood for advance infantry training. Eventually, he became a rifleman in Alpha Company, 1st Battalion, 3rd Brigade, 25th Infantry Division, Joel ended up floating face down in a rice paddy in the Central Highlands of Vietnam, an enemy bullet having entered his head behind his ear, just below the rim of his steel pot helmet.

Bevins read about Joel's death a few weeks later, in the *Copperfield Gazette*, and grieved mightily as he once again read "The American Scholar."

A Shape Shifter Goes to College

@ Howl Community College, Ashland, Ohio

By Courtney Rene

Based on a storyline from the novel *A Howl in the Night Part 4: Daybreak*, Rogue Phoenix Press, 2019

...From there, I went over to the Community College. I figured if I were out to change my future, now was as good a time as any. I didn't have an appointment, and I didn't really have a plan, but I figured–why not?

I stepped inside an old brown brick building that smelled a bit like dirt and mold. It felt cool within the walls. I didn't have any idea where to go. Thankfully, a dark-haired boy about my own age walked toward me in the dimly lit hallway. "Excuse me," I said.

He stopped. He focused in on me. His face bloomed into an enormous toothy smile. The smile made me hesitate. It was creepy. "Um...is there an office here?" I didn't have any experience at colleges. I didn't know if they had a main office or not.

"Sure, I'll take you over," he said and reached out to take my arm.

I stepped back just out of reach and turned in the direction he was pointing and said, "Great! Lead the way." I added in a smile to alleviate the possible insult of not wanting him to touch me.

His smile stayed in place. As it was giving me the willies, I wasn't certain that was a good thing. "My name's Brad," he said.

"Abby," I replied. I had a moment of worry that maybe I should have used a fake name. Then I let it go, since there had to be plenty of Abbys in the world.

He chatted me up on the short walk to the administration building with the usual questions: "Are you from here? Are you thinking of going to school here? What will you study?" I tried to answer simply, but politely, all the same.

Finally, he said, "Here you go." We were standing before a door that said, simply, *Admissions*. Awesome.

"Thanks," I said and turned to leave him where he stood.

I wasn't fast enough. He stopped me by taking my hand and saying, "I'll wait here for you."

Great.

I stepped through the door and to the first desk, where an older woman sat. Her brown hair was up in a sloppy bun that worked for her. She wasn't skinny, but not overly overweight either. She was dressed simply but professionally, and her genuine smiling face made it easier to approach her. "Hi," I said, "I'm interested in taking some classes in animal science. Is there someone I can speak to?"

"I'm sorry, but as we are in the summer session, we are short staffed in that department. However, they will be back in August. I can schedule an appointment for you and I'm sure we can get you set up and going before fall session begins. And you can also set up an appointment over in the Testing Center for your academic placement tests, career pathways recommendation assessment, and our institutional total quality survey! Oh, be sure to fill out the FFSA online so you can apply for financial aid."

Disappointment felt heavy on my heart for a moment, but I pushed it aside. I was a bit overwhelmed by all the steps it took to attend school, but whatever. It wasn't a wasted trip. It was a start. I quickly made an appointment with a counselor for August, said goodbye, and left the office. I thought I might take a little tour of the campus, maybe get a soda at the Student Union if it was open, and then go by the Testing Center to make other appointments. And I made a quick note on my phone to check into that FHA or FFA or FFSA thing.

Then, I stepped right into Brad. Ugh. I'd already forgotten him. "Oh, Brad. Sorry, I didn't see you there."

He laughed this throaty sound that felt dark and slimy. It slithered down my spine and settled in my gut. I had a feeling he'd intentionally stepped into me, just for the chance to have my body against his, no matter that it was only for a moment. "No problem."

I tried to step around him, but he again took my hand. He really needed to stop doing that. "Can I have your number? I'd love to go out sometime."

Awkward...and no. "I'm sorry, Brad. You seem really nice, but I have a boyfriend."

His hand holding mine tightened its grip. Painfully. I tried to wiggle it out, but the struggle just made him hold tighter. "You're lying," he said and tried to pull me in closer.

I moved as far back from him as I could, all the while I tried to get my hand free. "No. I'm not. I really do appreciate your help, though."

He stepped back in close to me.

I edged away again, and he came forward, until my back was against the wall across from the admissions door. Could the woman inside see us? I craned my neck around to try to see into the window of the door, but the angle was wrong. If I couldn't see in, she certainly couldn't see me.

I felt my wolf get testy. More of an annoyed feeling than angry. That all changed in a heartbeat the moment Brad pushed the length of his body up against mine and shoved his head and face a breath away. "Let go and back off," I growled. The sound of my voice should have been warning enough, but apparently Brad was not all that smart.

"No," he said and tried to press his lips against mine.

Oh, hell no. That was both a human and wolf response. Although I couldn't exactly shift into full wolf right there in the building hallway, I could pull the strength of the wolf forward. It wouldn't be the same as being a wolf, but it should be enough to teach him a lesson.

I reached down with my one free hand and grabbed a very tender spot on his body and...squeezed. Then I said, "I don't think you heard me, Brad. Let. Go."

The instant intake of a harsh breath was all the proof I needed, that I had his full attention. His hand instantly released mine and he tried to step away. As I had a hold of a very dear part of him, he couldn't do so.

I leaned forward so that I could whisper in his ear, more for dramatic affect than for fear of anyone hearing. Then I said, "Women don't like to be handled like that, Brad." I punctuated my words with a bit of a squeeze. He stopped breathing for a moment. I must admit I was enjoying myself. "You should know, I will be coming to this school. I really like the campus, and most of the people I've met. If I hear even an inkling of a rumor that you are treating anyone, girl or boy, with less than the respect they deserve, I will hunt you down and finish this little thing we have going

125

on right now." I again gave him a squeeze.

He had blue eyes. I hadn't realized it until then. Maybe it was because they were as big as saucers at that moment, but regardless, I had his full attention. "Do you understand me, Brad." It felt good to know I was able to take care of myself on my own. I was in control. It was a heady feeling.

He nodded his head.

I could have made him say it. It would have been easy, but I figured I'd won. I didn't need to rub his face in it any more than I already had. "Good," I said and released him.

He immediately stepped away from me. He didn't stop, either. He turned and hurried away without another glance or another word. I watched him move past another building–I noticed the sign said *Testing Center*. Good. Well, Brad, oddly enough, even in his current condition, helped to show me where the building was located! I laughed. The sound echoed down the hall almost like it was chasing him away. Boys. Shifter or just human, they were all the same.

Smiling to myself, I headed toward the snack bar in search of a cold drink. Then I would stop at the Testing Center before heading home. It'd been a good day. I was really looking forward to attending college.

About the Author

Jeffrey Ross, who resides in Arizona, is a writer, rock musician, and former full-time community college teacher. He has had four "Views" pieces published on *InsidehigherEd.com,* has authored and co-authored several national and international op-ed articles on community college identity, purpose, and culture, and has published numerous parody poems and articles on the *Cronk News* higher education satire website. Ross co-authored the comic and critically acclaimed campus novel *College Leadership Crisis: The Philip Dolly Affair* (Rogue Phoenix Press, 2011). He also authored the romance parody *Love in the RV Park: A Romance for Men* (Rogue Phoenix Press, 2013), the nonfiction life history about 1920s life in Scottsdale, AZ *Silent Sonora* (Rogue Phoenix Press 2015), a mature romance *The Auroran: Cold Front Redemption* (Rogue Phoenix Press 2016), and the thoughtful policy proposal *1040 Taxes Could be Replaced by One-Cent Fees!* (Rogue Phoenix Press 2018).

Silent Sonora

Silent Sonora details the life of a heroic young girl, Lillian Carroll, whose family resides in two tents during the 1920's and 1930's. Set in depression-era Scottsdale Arizona, this true story reveals Lillian's daily life experiences, the family's struggles, and her quest for a better life through education. Lillian tells readers directly about tent life, the local "emerging" Arizona communities, and the ongoing hardships she and her family confront. Both of Lillian's parents are deaf—her father works in the local agricultural industry, while her strong-willed mother endeavors to make the best home she can for her children. Lillian admits that "life was tough," but assures us she and her family had good times, too. Ultimately, Lillian's desire for a better education helps her situation—her love of family and strong faith give her the support she needs to finally gain independence.

Introduction

How many folks do you know who grew up living in a tent down in hot and dusty old Arizona? That's how we lived in the early days. You will soon learn about my family and me.

Earliest Memories

I was born Lillian Ruth Carroll, daughter of Fred W. Carroll and Cora Birchett Carroll, in Scottsdale, Arizona, on October 26, 1922. I spent my early childhood in Scottsdale, but we also lived in Laveen and Chandler during 1928-1929. During those years, my two brothers, Jim and Pete, worked with my father setting out citrus trees and irrigating the trees from wooden irrigation ditches. We moved back to Scottsdale in 1929 for a short time. My father would still drive back and forth to Laveen to work. Then, in 1930, we headed back to Laveen and lived in our family tent near the citrus fields. At this time, father would sometimes drive his Model A car over to Tempe to buy our groceries.

Laveen

Not much was going on in Laveen when my dad was working in the local agricultural "industry." Lots of alfalfa and grain fields covered the areas surrounding Laveen. I remember very clearly seeing wooden irrigation ditches back in 1928. The wood was wedged into the ditch, almost in the same style as the concrete-sided ones today. Now, they have concrete sheets or sides where the wood once was. Men would use sheets of canvas to raise the water level so they could irrigate the fields. In the summers, we would love to get in the cold, clear, well water in the wood ditches and jump and splash and have fun.

In town, the clerk who worked in the Laveen grocery store always kept an eye on me. He didn't have anything else to occupy him, I guess, so he really scrutinized the customers. What do you suppose he hoped to see?

When I was very small, I attended elementary school in Laveen. Many Mexican children went to our school. Quite a few buildings made up the school. We rode the school bus each morning. Occasionally, the kids in Laveen were pretty rough. I remember the time a group of boys started pushing my brother John around inside the bus on the way home. They picked him up and threw him into the front door of the bus, where the steps are located. He was bruised pretty badly. My brother Pete found out who did it, found the kid, and beat the tar out of him. Then the principal got a hold of Pete and gave him a whipping. When my dad found out, he went looking for the principal. Well, Mr. Principal holed up for a while until the crisis ended. Nothing came out of this, I guess. My father didn't know who the principal was or what he looked like. My mother was upset, too, but the beatings stopped at Pete. Probably a good thing, looking back. Justice could be "tough."

The second time we lived in Laveen, we set up our tent near a little butte. We would walk behind the hill, and we'd pretend we were traveling to distant, exotic places. We'd get our water from the neighbors, and they would also give us milk.

Brother Pete played quite a trick on those neighbors. He intentionally let their dog go loose. Then he caught the dog and took him back to the owner. She gave him five dollars for returning the dog. He did that twice. Then he decided she might wise up, so he quit.

Sky Harbor Airport

For a while, in 1931, we lived in our tent near the airport in Phoenix. We lived by Sky Harbor mostly because my father wanted to spend time near his sisters, Lodia and Alma, who resided close to us. At Sky Harbor, we lived near a big ditch, and we went swimming frequently. The ditch contained numerous squirming fish. We could see them jumping, jumping right out of the water. Once some workers drained the canal and we caught a "mess" and put 'em in a big tub. My mother cooked most of those fish, but what we couldn't eat, she fed to our chickens.

I remember hearing very noisy planes at Sky Harbor Airport. We noticed a few air shows, too, parachutists and such, but I never visited the airport to meet anybody or to watch planes fly in. I'm not sure if those notions ever occurred to me.

Why We Settled in Scottsdale

In 1932, we returned to stay, at least till 1940, in Scottsdale. But we still moved frequently, and we lived in different structures, from tents, to trailers, to adobes, to wood frame structures.

I have read a few stories by Louis L' Amour about the Wild West. All shooting, and romance, and adventure. All that beautiful scenery. Why did we come to the Phoenix area for our western adventure? Was my father afraid of mean things going on in the rest of the West? Our family heard about horrible events in Mesa, about a rape and lynching, and crimes occurring in other parts of Arizona and the Valley. But I never did understand why dad settled in Scottsdale. I do know dad liked Scottsdale because other people from Arkansas were living in town. He felt safer in this town than way out in the "Wild West." He felt close to these people.

Scottsdale

Back then, in the 30's, Scottsdale Road was paved downtown only.

North, where we lived, this "main street" was gravel. We saw and heard the iron-wheeled trucks moving up and down Scottsdale Road. Whenever they would go past our tent, the ground would rumble. In fact, the ground seemed to shake for several blocks. Quite a few horse and buggy rigs and bicycles could still be seen. Indians, with horse-drawn wagons, always came into Scottsdale to do their shopping and to sell items. Of course, more and more cars were appearing. The city didn't have any sidewalks, and we didn't have any fire hydrants, or a fire department.

When I was very little, cowboys were still driving cattle through downtown Scottsdale. Thinking back, seems like we still saw cattle drives occasionally into the early 40's. When the cattle would come through, you'd have to move. Pronto. Quickly. Often, a cattle drive would take quite a few hours to get through town. Buses and cars and trucks would simply have to stop. The cattle always had the "right of way." Cowboys and their always-noisy cattle covered the street. Of course, all those cows left a mess behind, too, a mess the people in town would eventually have to clean up. Just think of the problems such an environmental mess would cause nowadays. Cowboys were apparently taking the herds up north of Scottsdale to various ranches. I don't know where the cattle came from or what ranchers owned them. But some days, they seemed to be everywhere.

Quite a few wild horses galloped across the countryside just north of Scottsdale. They would congregate in places where water and grass were available. Various adults in town warned us kids about getting too close to the horses, if we should see any roaming the streets or roads. I never saw any wild horses within Scottsdale, but we did see a few on the outskirts.

Town was actually pretty bare. Many homes had outhouses. No traffic lights were installed in Scottsdale until the 50's. Only weekly newspapers, like the *Scottsdale Progress,* were available. But the *Progress* just carried local news. We had airplanes flying overhead, but they looked more like training planes than airliners. No trains came to Scottsdale, and buses just passed on through.

Salt River

The Salt River wasn't bridged on Scottsdale Road, nor was any ferry operating, because there wasn't enough water. At times, people would try to cross the river in a wagon or horse, but not too often. I don't remember seeing any boats. The river was about two feet deep, I guess. The Salt would run almost throughout the year, with a significant volume of water, but the river was usually shallow. Hundreds of trees grew right down to the water's edge. Many were cottonwoods.

We would go down to the beaches and have picnics. People would fish and catch catfish and suckers. My parents told us to stay away from the river because they didn't want us to drown. But the family would go down frequently and camp under the old bridge for a couple of days. Camping was fun, always fun. The new bridge was built in the 30's, but none of my family worked on that job. In the 40's, the Salt pretty much stopped flowing, since the Salt River Project had the river under control with dams upstream.

My father used to drive over to Tempe's Hayden Mills to get groceries and flour, but he never took me along. Indians would go to the mill in their wagons to pick up grains. Dad still made the trip to Tempe to buy groceries when we lived in Laveen for a while, back in the early 30's. Groceries were always cheaper in Tempe.

Critters

Oh, we had bobcats, scorpions, snakes, coyotes, and other critters that bit and stung. But varmints and vermin weren't a big deal. One time, my hand was hurting because a scorpion stung me, so I stuck my whole arm in a ditch to cool it off. That was all I needed to do. The pain went away after a bit. My brother Clifford got stung by a scorpion once, too, but mother just took care of him. He was fine.

I heard of people being struck by rattlesnakes, but I never knew anyone close to our family who had been bitten. Grandpa Carroll had to chop up a rattler with a hoe one day, but that was when we were living down in Chandler, about 10 miles south of Scottsdale. We really scattered after I spotted the snake.

Mr. Charles Miller

Do you know where O'Malley's lumber used to be, right close to the

Arizona Canal on Scottsdale Road? We had a home in the Miller's orchard. Mr. Miller was a good man, sort of a famous man, who did a lot for the town. Charles Miller had large tracts of property, mostly pasture for cows, citrus orchards, and alfalfa fields, in a large area between Indian School Road close to Scottsdale High and near the Arizona Canal.

His property was in the Camelback Road area. The Millers had a nice large home right on the corner of Indian School and Scottsdale Road. Mr. Miller had a family and children. I know he had a son named Bill. Their family was pretty well off. The Millers had newer cars. They lived in an orange grove, but we lived among the grapefruit trees and a few lemon trees.

Mr. Miller and my dad always got along pretty well. He would come to our tent and get my dad to work for him. They were very much alike, and they loved to play tricks on each other. Mr. Miller trusted my dad. In fact, when dad passed away in the 70's, he had the reputation of being the most honest man in Scottsdale.

They even raised a big pig together one time, and we all ate the pig at a roast. I don't know if the pig had a name, but he sure was a good-tasting pig. The bacon was flavorful.

Quick Reflections

We had no electricity. Earlier, we lived near the doctor's clinic in the olive trees, near a ditch right next to the road. We lived by the ditch when I was about six, about 1928. A cotton field flourished next to us. Goldwater's department store was across from the canal, but I don't remember ever shopping there as a child.

Thomas Road

You know Thomas Road? Well, back then, nothing was on Thomas Road. I mean nothing, just a road through the desert. People would dump trash and junk along Thomas. Piles of trash collected everywhere, just behind the creosote bushes, just back off the road. People would take their wagons, fill them with trash from their households, and just dump all kinds of stuff a few yards back from the travel way, not even out of sight.

That's where my dad found pieces of junk and materials to bring home. He also found scrap aluminum and copper and iron in the desert junk piles. Such a mess was amazing. Eventually, the city put a stop to dumping. This was back about 1927, when the area was quite an eyesore. I can still remember how dad would run over tin cans, and he'd get a stick to pry the cans off the wagon wheels.

Earl's Market and Groceries

Earl's Market, on Scottsdale Road, was the first grocery store in Scottsdale. A hotel and a few small rooms and apartments for rent were located above the market. As might be expected, a stairway went up to the hotel, and the rooms were much like small apartments. Who stayed in those rooms above Earl's Market? Well, tourists would come and rent rooms for their vacations. Tourists came out to see beautiful mountains, cowboys, and horses. People made arrangements in the grocery store to stay at the hotel.

My Aunt Lodia, Uncle Hayes, and their boys stayed at Earl's for a while when they first came to Scottsdale. A few of mother's friends would stay in the hotel while visiting.

Behind Earl's was the garage. Across the street was Scotty's Shop where workers did welding jobs. I used to enjoy watching the men pitch horseshoes behind the shop. We'd watch horseshoe games on the way home from school.

My mom would only go downtown with my father. Frequently, I would get to go along too. My mother didn't like to shop very much. She left most "trading" up to my dad.

I recollect going inside Earl's Market when I was very young. The store wasn't very big. Seems to me it was much like the size of a large classroom. A ceiling fan hung overhead, and the clerk was always close at hand to pick out or reach items for customers. Earl's had counters, and shelves, mostly behind the counters, kind of like a modern-day meat counter. Food stuffs were kept in large jars, like great big jars of pickles. Earl's sold those big pickles for five cents. I ate a few of them.

Anderson's Market came in a few years after, in the late 30's. My father traded more at Anderson's because he knew Mr. Anderson from the old days back in either Indiana or Arkansas. He was one of dad's old pals.

Grocery stores didn't have any way of keeping produce fresh back then. My dad would always check the merchants to find almost-spoiled produce because he could get really good deals. Sometimes, the markets would let my father know when they had produce which was about to spoil. One Saturday, Earl's Market gave us a box full of too-ripe bananas. They didn't last long at home. In just a few minutes, the bananas were gone, all eaten up.

More Scottsdale Life

Scottsdale had an icehouse, too, but I don't know how they made ice. Surely, they must have had electricity. Parts of downtown did have electric power, which must have come from Phoenix.

Scottsdale had a post office and a JP court, but the town didn't have a jail. Prisoners had to be taken to Tempe. A famous murder occurred while we were living in Miller's orchard when a so-called "retarded" person killed another man. A fellow had been teasing the "retarded" person unmercifully, so the "retarded" individual finally picked up an object and hit his tormenter and killed him on the spot. This murder made big news because things were usually so quiet and dull in Scottsdale. Nothing ever happened in town. I remember when my brother told us about the murder. I was small then, but Pete was quite excited.

Doctors, Midwives, and Health Care

Scottsdale had one doctor in town in those early days. His name was Dr. White, and he had his clinic right in the downtown area. Townspeople liked him. We never went to see him, though. One year, he had a huge Christmas party for everybody in town. He had a big, oh, kind of pine tree, all decorated. Grownups handed out little candies for the kids. That was fun.

When sister Nellie was about to be born, Dad called a young doctor from Tempe to come over and help with the delivery. I don't remember his name. I guess he was on call for the county. He is the one who, we believe, injured my little sister Nellie. After that incident, mother didn't trust young doctors.

Our regular doctor, Dr. Patterson, wasn't very young.

Dr. Patterson was our family doctor for several years. I guess he delivered most of us. He had an office in Tempe, but we never went to his office. Back then, he came to see us. He suffered from the shakes. Maybe he had the palsy and the twitches. I always wondered how he could see to drive and to deliver babies. But he was a very good doctor.

Mrs. Cruz used to help deliver children, babies. She was a midwife and helped Dr. Patterson with several of my mother's babies. Yes, all of mom's children were born at home. Mrs. Robinson was a midwife too. Our midwives were pretty smart. For example, they used a tea to cure infant jaundice. The midwives didn't stay at the house very long. They just made sure babies were born safely.

Of course, men folk cleared out of the house almost immediately when births occurred. I believe they were afraid of accidentally hurting the newborns. My father would come in several times a day to check on mother and a new child, but he wouldn't touch the baby for a long time. We kids would help, but the midwife always took charge.

I don't know about how much trouble was related to childbirth back then, but my mother didn't seem to have many difficulties.

The kids did, though. My sister Nellie, who died of coronary and lung problems as a young adult, had been injured during birth. She couldn't sit up until she was two years old. My brother Paul died of pneumonia when he was only two weeks old, but that was back in Arkansas.

By the way, when I was born, I weighed four pounds. Mother said I was a fat baby.

More on Doctoring and Healthcare

My mother tended not to go to the doctor's, since she always thought such care cost too much. Dad also avoided the doctor's office. On one of his annual firewood cutting trips, he accidentally cut his foot with either a saw or an ax. I understand his cut bled profusely since the wound was pretty bad, but he took care of that gash with his first aid kit. Within a month he was okay. He just didn't have the time or inclination to visit the doctor's.

Dad always kept barbwire strung around the tent. I don't know if the barbwire was to keep out animals or people. But one time, Glen was chasing Jim all over the place and Jim ran into the barbwire, cutting his nose. Jim ended up going to the doctor. Dad took him, and Jim had to get several stitches in his nose.

When I was about fourteen, I broke my arm while playing baseball. I actually slipped on frost-covered grass. A doctor, not from Scottsdale, worked with the schools. He put a plaster cast on my broken arm. Boy. Somebody put ice on my arm to take the swelling down. My broken arm helped me to get out of lots of work, though.

College Leadership Crisis: The Philip Dolly Affair

A Crisis in Community College Leadership: The Phillip Dolly Affair is literary in development but grounded in "chaotic" community college daily experience. The novel is comic, satiric, quasi-politically correct, edgy, and richly descriptive of community college life, leadership foibles, and cultural themes. This hyperbolic text is entertaining, edifying, and fun. Little community college fiction—comic or otherwise—exists—the authors are fearless in their humorous—and sometimes biting—analysis of community college culture....

The "stereotype-busting" authors reacquaint readers with the [faded] ideals of the 1960's social renaissance.

While community colleges are currently receiving heightened attention, this novel provides a behind-the-scenes analysis of many "whispered truths," those simmering but unspoken workplace issues, behaviors, and machinations nearly every worker [Everyman] in America will recognize.

Love in the RV Park: A Romance for Men

This quirky and fast moving romance revolves around passionate lovers in tangled and mostly unfulfilling relationships. The tale is complete with hot housewives, rock musicians, exotic dancers, motorcycles, steamy nail polish-melting love scenes, hard drinking college professors, hybrid alien children, a romantic bug exterminator, girl fights, a New Year's Eve brawl, religious zealotry, prophecies (The Temple of Just DOET)—and more. Ultimately, Love in the RV Park is about the male perception (misperception?) of the female psyche—and the novel attempts to answer an age-old question: What do women want? Laugh or cry—you'll come away enlightened after reading this zany romance.

The Auroran: Cold Front Redemption

August Nightingale, in late middle age, has had little success with relationships-- and not much meaningful satisfaction in the world of work. Abruptly deciding to "leave it all behind," he embarks on a snowy road trip to visit Civil War battlefields in Pennsylvania. His journey becomes one of self-realization. A mishap on the highway, the kindness of his beautiful neighbor Sarah (who helps him to convalesce), and the friendly people of Aurora change his life and his heart. This mature romance novel shows that it is never too late to find happiness, to experience meaningful love, when souls are honest and open to the truths of human experience.

1040 Taxes Could be Replaced by One-Cent Fees!

1040 culture—like it or not—exists because the United States government taxes personal income to raise trillions to fund the federal treasury. This amount will undoubtedly increase in the future—but so will American commerce and the GDP. The focus of this book will be how we can raise 3.5 or 5.0 or 6 trillion dollars efficiently and accurately while eliminating the unwieldy 1040 tax return process. The TFP plan, basically, is to "automatically" assess a 1 cent fee (.01 dollar) on all trackable transactions in the US (or related international transactions using American financial institutions). Say good bye to tax preparation, deductions, refunds, credits—this will be a pay-as-you-go system. Tax audits and tax-related stress will become history.